SWAMP CAT

SWAMP CAT

By Jim Kjelgaard

Illustrated by Edward Shenton

DODD, MEAD & COMPANY

NEW YORK

© 1957 by Jim Kjelgaard

Tenth Printing

Library of Congress Catalog Card Number: 57-10167

Printed in the United States of America
by The Cornwall Press, Inc., Cornwall, N. Y.

To Polly Goodwin

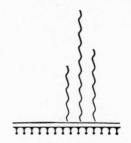

CONTENTS

CONTENTS

SWAMP CAT

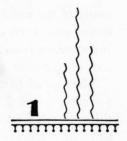

1

EXILED

The sound came to Frosty as a mere vibration that hummed about the fine hairs in his inner ears and set his whiskers to tingling. About to leap from the shelf on which he crouched and resume the boisterous play with his two brothers, he remained where he was and strained for a repetition of the noise. He knew only that it was. Before he could continue playing, he must know what it was.

On the chaff-littered floor of the shed in which they lived, Frosty's brothers engaged in a mock war. They slapped and bit each other, but their claws were sheathed and needle-sharp baby teeth did not penetrate the skin. Breaking, they raced pell-mell across the shed. So nearly alike that no casual observer could have seen any difference between the pair, one gray kitten stretched full-length behind a little heap of chaff and waited in this cunning ambush for the other to venture near.

They too would have stopped playing if they had been

aware of the noise, but only Frosty knew it because only his senses were keen enough to detect it. However, more than just superior powers of perception set him apart from the kittens on the floor.

The mother of the three, beloved pet of the household, was a medium-sized gray cat that had never done much of anything except doze in the sunshine in summer, lie beside the stove in winter, rub against the legs of the various members of the family when she was pleased, sulk when she was not, and somewhat indifferently carry on various affairs which no cat ever considers the business of any human. Their father was a huge black-and-white old tom. A confirmed wanderer and unregenerate adventurer, he bore as many battle scars as any soldier ever carried. Smart and crafty, he had never offered allegiance to anything save his own wanderlust and he feared nothing.

From point of lineage or breeding, neither the gray mother nor the black-and-white old tom were distinguished by anything special. Products of generations of cats that had been allowed to wander where they would and breed as they pleased, in local parlance, they were just common cats.

It was a misnomer, though, because there is no such thing as a common cat. Perhaps because they were a little nearer the source of things, the ancient peoples who brought cats from the wilderness to their firesides understood this perfectly. They knew that cats are proud. They applauded their intelligence, warmed to their complex characters, marveled at their temperaments and tried eagerly to fathom that unfathomable mystery, so that they might understand why cats were as they were. Failing, they accepted their failure with wisdom.

They could not understand cats any more than they could

understand why gold glittered or precious jewels sparkled, but they did not have to know why a flawless diamond or ruby came about in order to appreciate it. They bowed to perfection and they acknowledged the perfection of cats by making them their equals, or even their superiors. Cats had first choice at their own tables, and whole villages walked in the funeral procession when a cat died. They made cats the companions of kings, and it was death to the commoner who hurt or even touched one. They put cats in their temples and worshipped them; many a figure which meant a god to these ancient peoples wore the head of a cat on the body of a man.

Some part of what had impressed these ancients was evident in Frosty as he lay on the shelf and waited for the sound to repeat itself, so he could identify it. Though he gave his entire being to the task at hand, his was not the strained tension of a dog that concentrates completely on just one thing. Rather than fret toward the source of the sound, it was as though Frosty had opened an invisible door which not only could but must let the source become one with him.

Blood brother to the two kittens on the floor, Frosty was a third bigger than they. But the lithe slimness of his mother had tempered the blocky proportions of his father, so that he combined size with strength and fluid grace. His basic fur was jet black, but single white hairs were so scattered through it that he looked as though he were sprinkled with hoarfrost. His eyes were remarkable, and somehow seemed to reflect the accumulated wisdom of all cats since the first.

A split second after the first tremor, the noise came again, a tiny bit louder, and thereafter resolved itself into a pattern of rhythmic noises. A horse was coming, and because the

tremors strengthened with each step it took, Frosty knew
that it was coming toward the shed.

Finally becoming aware of the sound, the gray kittens
stopped playing until they too could identify it. Frosty's eyes
sparkled mischievously. He had been born with a quivering
bump of curiosity that stopped throbbing only when it was
satisfied, and it was satisfied only when Frosty knew at all
times exactly what lay about him. His nose was relatively
dull, but his eyes and ears verged on the marvelous, so he
interpreted the world keenly through sight and hearing. But
once he was sure, as he was now sure that he heard a horse,
he need concern himself no longer because, from this point
on, that part of his brain which worked automatically would
take over and tell him what the horse was doing.

Imps of mischief continued to dance in Frosty's eyes. Having just detected the sound, his brothers must now identify
it. Trying to do so was occupying all their attention and
there would never be a better chance to take them off guard.
Frosty launched himself from the shelf.

It was a kitten's leap, propelled by a kitten's muscles, but
there was still something breath-taking, almost unreal, about
it. No blind jump, every nerve and muscle in Frosty's body
was at all times under perfect control. He landed exactly
where he had planned on landing, astride his two brothers,
and the three kittens tumbled over and over on the floor.

Even while he parried paw or fangs, or inflicted playful
blows of his own, that part of his brain which had taken
over for Frosty kept him informed of the horse's progress.
There was no need to stop playing and give the horse undi-
vided attention. Horses, in a cat's opinion, were big, clumsy
and uninteresting. The horse stopped near the house to

which the shed belonged and a man whose voice Frosty did not recognize called,

"Halloo the house!"

The door opened and the mistress of the place answered, "Hello, Luke. Just a minute."

When the house door opened, at once the two gray kittens broke off playing and padded to the shed's door. They stood before it, voicing little mews of anticipation and so eager that their heads alternately raised and dipped, then turned, as though on swivels. Their tails were straight and pink tongues flicked out.

Though he did not hide his interest, Frosty stayed well back from the shed door. He knew as well as his two brothers did that the saucers of milk and occasional pile of table scraps upon which all three kittens fed came from the house and that the woman always brought them. But Frosty possessed in full a quality which his brothers had only in part.

Frosty's heritage, in great measure, came from his renegade father. Incapable of fearing anything, he was sufficient unto himself and he'd known that from the first day he'd opened his eyes and looked around the shed. There was not and never would be a situation with which he could not cope or a foe from whom he would run in panic. His self-confidence was almost as vast as his curiosity. He would stand alone, or with kindred spirits. Never would he place himself at the mercy of, or pay homage to, one who was not kindred.

He liked the woman. She was unfailingly kind and gentle. She knew exactly how to pet him and she—a small point— brought his food. But he would not, as the gray kittens did, unbend so far as to meet her at the door. She was not his superior.

The woman spoke again and there was a little question in her voice. "Mr. Harris isn't here now, Luke, but I suppose it's all right for you to take them?"

"It's all right, Miz Harris." The man's voice was curiously flat and toneless. "I tol' the Mister I'd get 'em today."

"Well—" The woman still doubted. "How much did he promise you?"

"Two dollars, Miz Harris."

"All right. I'll pay you. They're in here."

She pulled the shed door open and Frosty looked out to see his mistress standing beside a lean hillman, dressed in sun-faded blue trousers that, somehow, were kept from falling down by frayed galluses draped over a torn shirt. The man's hair needed cutting and ragged sideburns strayed down either cheek, to meet beneath his chin. His face was hatchet like, its distinguishing characteristic being a pair of pale blue eyes. He held the reins of a skittish-looking brown horse that wore a good saddle.

Frosty stayed where he was, instinctively flattening himself so that he lay a little nearer the floor. Tails erect, eyes happy, pleased purrs filling the shed, the two gray kittens arched against their mistress' feet. She knelt and took one in either hand.

"Oh, the dears! I hate to see them go!"

"Kind o' hard," the man said, "to keep so many cats in town."

"It's impossible," she sighed. "Can you wait a while? It lacks an hour to their feeding time, but maybe I should feed them before they go?"

"Now don't you fret," he reassured her. "In two hours I'll have 'em up at my place, an' anybody in the hills'll tell you Luke Trull's critters don't starve. They'll eat plenty."

"I hope so. How are you going to carry them?"

"If you'll just hold Queenie—"

He handed the horse's reins to her, took a gunny sack from beneath his shirt, plopped the two surprised gray kittens into it and advanced on Frosty. Unafraid, but always willing to temper valor with discretion, Frosty waited until he was near enough to swoop, then darted into a cracked piece of tile pipe that lay in the shed. Luke Trull said,

"This'n ain't friendly."

"No," Mrs. Harris admitted, "he isn't like the others."

"Makes no diffe'nce. We can use him, an' his wildness might pay off up in the hills."

Frosty readied himself. The three-foot length of tile was not merely the best but almost the only hiding place in the shed. If he was found out here, he'd have no choice except fighting. Luke Trull's hand crept like an unwieldy snake into the hollow tile and Frosty struck with unsheathed claws. The man gritted,

"Why, ya leetle—!"

"What's wrong?" the woman asked anxiously.

"The leetle—! He bit me!"

"Please be gentle!"

The hand came nearer and its steel-strong fingers enfolded Frosty. The black kitten raked until his paws were secured and then scissored with needle-sharp baby teeth. Spitting and snarling, he was pulled out of the tile and dropped into the gunny sack, along with his brothers. He made another mad lunge at Luke Trull but succeeded only in entangling his claws in the sacking. Furious, but unable to do anything about it at once, Frosty subsided.

The man held up his scratched hand. "The leetle—!"

The woman said, "I'm sorry!"

"Makes no mind," Luke Trull said. "I'll stop down to the drugstore an' git aught to put on it."

"I'll pay for it. Will two dollars extra be all right?"

"If ye've a mind, Miz Harris."

"You—you won't hurt the kittens?"

"Oh no, Miz Harris! 'Course not! Why would I hurt 'em when I told the Mister I'd take 'em?"

"Here's your money."

"Thankee."

Luke Trull tied the mouth of the gunny sack, slung it over the saddle horn, and swung expertly into the saddle. The horse broke into a fast walk and the gunny sack bobbed back and forth in cadence with the horse's movements. Paws spread, claws extended, Frosty steadied himself by holding onto the sacking. One of the gray kittens whimpered plaintively. Rigid with uncertainty, the second merely stared. Frosty paid his brothers not the slightest attention.

He could smell nothing, see nothing except dim light that filtered through the gunny sack's coarse weave, and he heard little but the measured clomp-clomp of the horse's hooves. Since he could know nothing whatever of what lay about him, or what might happen next, he couldn't possibly plan any intelligent course of action or know how to cope with the next problem that arose. He must be ready for anything and he was.

Though he knew no fear, his nerves were taut as a blown-up balloon. From the tip of his nose to the end of his tail, no tiny part of him was even slightly relaxed. Just so, provision is made for all cats that find themselves in serious and uncertain situations. Frosty, and to a lesser extent the gray kittens, were ready to fly in any direction or to do instantly whatever the next second, the next minute, the next hour, or any elapsed time, might have them do.

They did not bob around as puppies would have because each had all four claws firmly fixed in the sacking and, in a very real way, even while they were together, they remained apart. Though on occasion several cats will cooperate to do what one alone cannot do, theirs is not the pack instinct of dogs and wolves. Intelligent enough to work with others when the situation demands it, they are too highly individualized to look to any one leader and too smart ever completely to trust their own fate to anything except themselves.

The gray kitten that had mewed before, called a second time. It was not a cry of fear, but one of appeal. Until now, the kitten's world had consisted of the shed, of daytime forays into the yard, of all the food it could eat and of unfailingly gentle treatment at the hands of human beings. The desperate kitten wanted only to be back in the familiar world from which it had been so rudely torn.

Far more intelligent and advanced than either of the gray kittens, Frosty gave himself wholly to facing things as they were, with no vain lamentations for what had been. Still able to smell only the dusty sack, to see little and to hear only the horse's hoofbeats, he kept every sense alert. Thus he knew when they left the road and started climbing a mountain path. The little dust bombs that had been exploding under the horse's feet no longer floated upwards. Metal-shod hooves rang on rocks and boulders and the air was cleaner.

Frosty sensed only the physical change, welcome because the dust was less oppressive. Being a cat, he knew nothing of the town's social life, as it was conducted by humans, and if he had known, he wouldn't have cared. But town life had a definite bearing on why he and his brothers were here.

The town owed its existence to the fact that it was the logical place to establish a railroad yard. Its inhabitants consisted of those who worked for the railroad and various business and professional people who had gathered to serve them. The first scheduled train had run over the new-laid rails just twenty-eight years ago, and, with few exceptions, everybody in the town who was past thirty had come from somewhere else. Those who'd stayed had established the town's oldest and most-respected families, and such traditions as there were centered about them and the history they'd seen in the making.

It was a colorful story, for though there hadn't been any town, there had been people here long before the steel rails crept this way. They were the Trulls, the Casmans, the Haroldsons, the Gates, and others. According to popular report, in which there was probably more than a little truth, these natives of the region lived back in the hills because no place that smacked even faintly of civilization would have them and, before the coming of the railroad and the building of the town, they did just about as they pleased. A choice story, one the town's newspaper reprinted at least once a year, concerned the twenty-five-year-long feud that the Trulls and Casmans had carried on with the Gates.

Occasionally, some of the hill people had come into town, worked on the railroad long enough to get money for some purpose or other and gone again. They hadn't wanted steady jobs and they still didn't.

Now the town's relations with the hill dwellers were somewhat curious. The railroad had brought law with it

and the hill people had had to conform, but they had never conformed completely. Periodically, the game warden found a Trull, Casman, or some other hillman, with game or fish taken out of season. Two years ago, federal officers, searching for illicit stills, had combed the whole area thoroughly. They had uncovered no bootlegging operations but that, as every townsman knew, was only because the hill dwellers had been too clever for them.

Legend and fact mingled indiscriminately to influence the town's view of the hill people. It was commonly believed that, once a hill man promised to do something, the deed was as good as done. It was also believed that, back in their own wild country, the hill dwellers were still a law unto themselves. Many were the darkly whispered tales of violence, even murder, and pagan rites. But most of these stories were born in some town-dweller's imagination.

However, there was fact, and Andy Gates furnished the outstanding example. Andy was the last resident survivor of the Gates clan. Three years ago, looking fourteen but claiming he was sixteen, Andy had come into town and obtained a job on the night shift in the roundhouse. Days he had enrolled in the town's high school, where he not only completed a four-year course in three but graduated as salutatorian. Then, though he might have continued to work for the railroad, with every prospect of some day having a very good job, Andy had gone back to the hills.

So fact and romance tinted each other, and when Mrs. Harris handed the three kittens over to Luke Trull, she hadn't the least idea that he would do anything but exactly as he had promised and give them a fine home. She didn't know anything about his home and had only a vague idea of where he lived. However, who could doubt that surplus kittens, for which there was no room in town, would be very well off in the hills? It never occurred to her, it never occurred to anyone outside the hills, that Luke was a man of the meanest order. With an inborn aversion to work, he liked money and he constantly schemed and planned to get some. His scratched hand, an injury not even worth noticing, he had quickly recognized as an opportunity to extort two dollars more from Mrs. Harris. He had never had the slightest intention of buying any antiseptic from the drugstore and now, as his horse climbed the mountain path, he looked for a good place to rid himself of the kittens. They'd be nothing except a burden at Luke's place and he did not want them.

At the same time, he must be very careful. Those fools

from town were always coming into the hills for one reason or another, and, of course, everybody in the town knew everybody else. If he were seen discarding the kittens, he'd get no more surplus kittens or pups either and thus a handy source of income would dry up.

Luke swung in the saddle to look behind him and saw nobody. There didn't seem to be anybody ahead, either, but Luke's were the senses and instincts of a hillman. He could not see around the next bend, but there might be somebody there who could see him. Luke rode on. He rounded the bend and silently commended himself for his own caution.

Swinging down a long, straight stretch toward him came young Andy Gates. Although of anything except a poetical turn of mind, Luke thought, as he always did when he saw Andy at a distance, of a birch sapling that has shot far into the air without developing a trunk that is capable of supporting it. There was nothing complimentary in the comparison; slim and tall saplings might topple with the first storm. But the description was apt. Six feet two, Andy's body had not yet filled out in proportion to his height. He had straight, jet-black hair and a smile that always seemed in bud on his mouth but never quite bloomed. Unless one looked squarely into his black eyes—and Luke never did because Andy's eyes made him uncomfortable—the over-all impression he gave was one of extreme gentleness. With his long legs, he covered the ground like a coursing greyhound. He was now, Luke guessed, on his way into town to buy some needed supplies. They met and Luke said,

"Hi, Andy."

Andy touched a hand to his forehead in salute. "Hello, Luke."

Then they passed and each continued his separate way. A puzzled smile parted Luke's thin lips.

Young Gates was a queer one. Smart enough, if book learning passed for smartness; he had gone to town and got himself a schooling. Then, and only he knew why, he had come back to the ancestral Gates holdings in Dog Tooth Valley. What he, or for that matter anyone else, wanted there was a mystery. There was some five hundred acres, all paid for and with a clear title. But there was not enough plow land to provide even a small family with enough vegetables for its own use. Here and there was a small patch of scrub timber, and almost all the rest was swamp land.

When they'd needed that above all else, Dog Tooth Valley had provided a safe haven for the once-numerous Gates men. They knew the only safe paths across their endless swamps and, to this day, nobody else did. But the feud was long since ended. Though it had been neither as prolonged nor as bitter as the town liked to remember it and there had been a lot more hand to hand slugging than there ever had been combat with deadly weapons, the law had ended it and a new day had come to the hills. It was a better day, too. Who but a fool would try to get what he wanted with a gun when it was much easier and safer to think his way through to it?

Turning to steal a covert glance behind him, Luke saw that Andy had disappeared. The man whirled his horse to the side of the trail, lifted the bag of kittens from his saddle horn and threw the still-tied sack into a copse of brush.

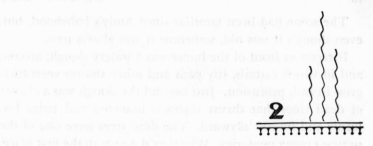

2

ANDY

The spring sun, which rose at half-past five, was just climbing into the sky when Andy Gates got out of bed. He entered the compact kitchen of his little house, started a wood fire in the range, put a pot of coffee over an open lid hole and, while waiting for this to start percolating, walked to the front of his place and looked over his domain.

The house was built on a rocky knoll, one of the few places in Dog Tooth Valley that was not given over to swamp land. Enough topsoil clung to the elevation to support a small garden. Surrounding the garden was a tightly woven picket fence, and, even as Andy watched, a trim doe from out of the swamp nosed hopefully at the pickets. Andy smiled with his eyes; the doe could not get into his garden. Beyond, were three small sheds. In one Andy kept the dozen chickens that supplied him with eggs and an occasional table fowl; the other two were a fur shed and a place for storing provisions. All the rest was swamp land.

The scene had been familiar since Andy's babyhood, but, even though it was old, somehow it was always new.

Directly in front of the house was a watery slough, around and in which cattails, lily pads and other swamp vegetation grew in lush profusion. Just beyond the slough was a cluster of dead trees that thrust skeleton branches and twigs forlornly and forever skyward. The dead trees were one of the swamp's many mysteries. Why they'd grown in the first place, Andy did not know. Nor could he understand why they did not fall down, as other dead trees did, sooner or later. He thought that they took out of the swamp some mineral content that toughened and hardened them. They'd been there since he could remember. Beyond the trees, marked here and there by other dead trees and an occasional knoll upon which grew a little patch of live ones, the swamp stretched clear to the foot of some low hills that rose in the distance. Andy picked out the paths across it; the sloughs and ponds wherein lurked pickerel, perch and bass; the game trails; and the places where, in bygone days, men of the Gates clan had hidden from their enemies.

He turned soberly back to the stove, put a slab of butter in a skillet, melted it and broke four eggs into it. He toasted bread on top of the stove and sat down to eat his breakfast.

The Gates family had long since scattered far and wide. When the railroad brought the law with it, they could no longer raid the Trulls and Casmans and retreat to the safety of their swamp. Safety was about all the swamp did offer; no hungry family had yet found a way to take a livelihood from it. Andy poured himself a second cup of coffee.

One by one, the Gates men had taken their belongings and their families from the hills. But there'd been the inevitable one who couldn't leave. Foolish, the rest had called Jared, Andy's father, but Jared hadn't cared. Only his son could understand that some roots went too deep to be torn out. Jared might have left the swamp, but he wouldn't have been happy elsewhere. This was perfectly plain to Andy because he wouldn't either. He'd striven to finish four years of high school in three largely because he was lonesome for the swamp and he'd gone to school for a specific purpose.

Jared, resting these past four years in the family plot on Fiddler's Knob, had been contented just to accept the swamp. He'd hunted a little, fished a little, trapped a little and worked by the day for whomever saw fit to give him a job. Andy wanted to make the swamp produce something worthwhile and he'd spent hours in the school library, seeking a way.

Farming, in the accepted sense, was not even to be considered. The swamp would grow no commercial crop. There was little likelihood that it contained valuable minerals, either, but, by sheer chance, Andy had run across an account of the great swamps of Louisiana and the muskrats that abounded there. In this, he hoped, he had his answer.

There were fur bearers in the swamp; mink, otter, raccoon and an occasional fox or coyote. Strangely enough, there were no muskrats, but Andy thought this was explained by the fact that all the swamp's outlets were subterranean. There was no surface connection with any stream or river, and any muskrat that tried to get into the swamp would have a long and perilous journey overland. However, he knew that there was a vast abundance of the aquatic plants on which muskrats fed, and muskrats did very well in northern climates, too. They were found well into Canada.

If Andy could establish muskrats in his swamp, let them

multiply and harvest the surplus, he might very well earn more than just a livelihood. At any rate, the experiment was worth trying and, after corresponding with various animal dealers and breeders, he had succeeded in buying six pairs of muskrats. If everything went according to schedule, they'd arrive on the one o'clock train.

Andy washed his breakfast dishes, tidied up the house and went outside. Hoisting a white tail over her back, the hopeful doe fled into the swamp. Andy walked toward his garden and was halted by a whirring rattle. A thick-bodied rattlesnake wriggled hastily out of his way and he let it go. Rattlesnakes were one commodity that the swamp did produce in abundance, and they'd killed all three of the dogs Andy had tried to keep. After that, he had stopped keeping them. There was little point in getting another dog when it was certain to run afoul of a snake and he didn't really miss the companionship. Though he lived alone, he was never lonely. Nobody could be if he loved and understood the swamp.

Opening the gate, Andy looked at his garden, saw that it had not been molested and sighed relievedly. Deer could not get through the fence, but raccoons had a fancy for tender young vegetables, too, and they could get over it. Perhaps the rattlesnake, dangerous only to the unwary and the small creatures upon which it lived, was acting as a sort of guardian. It would be a good idea to let it stay where it was. Catching up a hoe, Andy cultivated his young plants.

Two hours later, he laid the tool aside, returned to the house, took up a casting rod with a silver spoon on the leader and stepped down to the slough. He cast expertly, laying his spoon just off the fringe of lily pads that grew on the far side of the slough. He let the spoon sink a little ways, began the retrieve, and there was a succession of little ripples as a good bass followed it clear across the slough. Andy cast again and again. On his fourth cast, the bass struck. He fought it across the slough and lifted it out of the water. Thus he had his dinner. After he'd cooked and eaten it, he started down the trail leading into town.

Passing Luke Trull, he was happy to salute him briefly and hurry on. The feud was long since just a memory, but even if it had never been, Andy would not have liked Luke Trull. He was a coarse and often cruel man, and better left alone. Given to violent rages, he was, nevertheless, usually able to avoid trouble.

Andy strode into the town, returned the greetings of friends he met there, made his way to the express office and waited for Johnny Linger, the agent, to look up. An old friend from Andy's railroading days, Johnny's greeting was explosive,

"Hi, Andy!"

"Hello, Johnny. Is there anything for me?"

"Six somethings." Johnny indicated six small wooden crates at one side of the room. "I was hoping you'd drop by. What are they, Andy?"

"Muskrats." Andy peered between the slats of one crate at two brown-furred animals about as big as cottontail rabbits. "Six mated pairs."

Johnny asked whimsically, "What are you going to do with 'em, Andy?"

"See if they like my swamp. I forgot my pack board, Johnny. Will you loan me one?"

"Sure thing."

"Would you mind letting me pick them up after dark?"

"Any time you say. You'd just as soon keep it private, huh?"

"I'd just as soon," Andy agreed. "Nobody will know I have them if I take them in after dark."

A moment before the sack landed in the brush, all three kittens turned so that the entire trio landed on their feet. This was not an instinctive move but a planned one that was possible because a cat thinks so swiftly. They would not have been hurt if they'd been thrown on rocks.

As it was, the yielding branches of the brush broke their fall, so that they came to earth almost gently. Wild-eyed, panting, the two gray kittens stretched full-length and waited tensely. As tense as his brothers, Frosty was not satisfied merely to wait. A true son of the black-and-white tom, he had inherited all that old warrior's character, courage and spirit.

Before he did anything else, to the best of his ability, Frosty determined what lay about them.

Normally he depended on his ears, his eyes, and to a lesser extent, his nose. Now his eyes were almost useless, but the sun shone brightly and some light penetrated the sack. Just overhead, a leafy branch was moving in the gentle wind, and when the branch moved, its shadow shifted across the sack. Frosty studied it intently, trying to determine exactly what it was and why it should be. Unable to do so, after the shadow had moved back and forth a dozen times, he did satisfy himself that it was harmless. He then gave himself over to the use of his ears and nose.

Faintly in the distance, he still heard the measured hoof-beats of Luke Trull's horse. The animal was going farther away and therefore he need not concern himself with it,

but indelibly graven on Frosty's mind was the image of Luke
Trull himself. The man was a deadly enemy and had proven
himself such. He must never be considered as anything else,
but enemies could harm or be harmed only when they were
near and Luke Trull was gone with his horse. There were
more immediate problems.

For a short space the only sounds were the horse's hoof-
beats, the sighing of the gentle breeze and the kittens' panting. Then a mottled thrush that had been startled into
hasty flight when the hurled sack came his way, cocked his
head in the chokecherry tree to which he had flown. The
sack seemed harmless. At any rate, it did not pursue. Curious, the thrush flew back to the copse, tilted on a twig and
gave voice to a few questioning notes.

Frosty heard and interpreted correctly. He had seen birds
and even stalked them, when he and his brothers played
outside the shed. He was not particularly concerned about
the thrush. It was unlikely to offer a battle; all the birds
he'd ever seen had avoided him. Frosty started suddenly.

Winging in solitary flight over the mountain, a jet-black
crow voiced its raucous song. Frosty heard and marveled.
Never before had such a sound crossed his ears and he waited
to hear it again. When the crow did not repeat its call,
Frosty sank back. But he knew no peace. His curiosity,
aroused and unsatisfied, tormented him and would continue
to do so until he heard another crow call and identified the
source of a sound so intriguing.

The sun burned hotly and the gray kitten that had mewed
before, cried again. The weakest of the three, the kitten was
suffering far more than his brothers. Frosty looked once
toward his protesting brother and turned his head away. He
too was hungry and thirsty, but it was not in him to cry.

He poked experimentally at a tiny hole in the gunny sack. Unable to thrust his paw through, he turned his attention elsewhere. He was too smart to waste time trying the obviously impossible. When he laid plans, they would succeed.

The only scents that reached his nostrils were those of sun-warmed foliage and earth and the heavy, rank odor of a rotting log that lay nearby. The weakening gray kitten mewed again and Frosty twisted uncomfortably. It was long past feeding time and hunger was an ache. But thirst was becoming a torture.

The fine hairs in Frosty's inner ears quivered like stretched wires and he turned his head toward the rotting log. The sound that originated there was so faint and wispy that only a very sensitive ear could have detected it. A chipmunk ran up the log, saw the sack, stopped, sat up for a better view, squeaked in frenzied alarm and turned to flash back along the log. He dived into its hollow interior.

The weakening gray kitten twisted, laid his ears back, snarled and sprang upon and slashed viciously at his gray brother. The attacked kitten slashed back. Exhausted by its own tremendous effort, the feeble kitten sank down apathetically and closed its eyes. In a grim way, it was the luckiest of the three, for it would be the first to die.

Frosty unsheathed and sheathed his claws. He looked meaningfully at the second gray kitten, which flattened its ears and spat at him. Frosty turned around to face his brother.

The sun went down and when it did a chill fell on the mountain. But it brought no relief from raging thirst. though hunger was forgotten. The weakest kitten, past caring what happened, stretched limply. Its eyes were closed and it gasped for breath. But Frosty and the other gray kitten were still strong.

Far across the mountain, his every need and want attended to, Luke Trull slept soddenly in his comfortable bed.

Frosty strained. Something was walking nearby.

It walked on paws so soft and stealthy that the sound came to Frosty's ears almost like the ghost of a noise. It was less than half real, but it was there. Frosty turned to face it, knowing that, as always, he must be ready for anything. Nearby, there was a short sigh as something expelled its breath.

The gray kitten laid his ears back and snarled. Frosty caught the scent of whatever came and at once was aware of two things. The approaching creature was alien to him but he was immediately hostile to it. Somewhat like a dog, whatever came was not a dog. But it was wild and big, and it meant no good. Frosty bristled.

He could have no way of knowing that the creature, now smelling closely at the sack, was a prowling coyote. A big and crafty old male, the coyote had acquired his craft the hard way. Four years ago, he had left his right front paw in a steel trap, and ever since he had avoided everything which he did not know.

He knew all about helpless kittens and pups in gunny sacks. Over the years, Luke Trull had carried dozens from the town to a promised "good home" in the hills. It was one of the more paradoxical aspects of town-hill relationships that nobody had ever challenged him or stopped to think about it. The most superficial reasoning would have demonstrated that, if Luke had really taken home all the kittens and pups he had promised to take there, he couldn't possibly have room for anything else.

Luke's method of disposing of surplus kittens and pups was manna to the coyote. And, in a way, the coyote's very presence was a blessing to the helpless animals. The coyote killed cleanly, never needing more than one snap of his jaws, and such a death was much easier than waiting for thirst and hunger to do their work. Strong pups and kittens often lived a surprisingly long time.

Having satisfied himself that this was exactly what he had thought it would be, the coyote pinned the sack down with his front paws and went to work with his teeth. He had done this so many times that he was a past master at it and his technique was admirable. Rip a hole in the sack, pull out the trapped kittens or pups, snap once and enjoy an easy meal.

The coyote was neither in a hurry nor particularly concerned. This formula he himself had perfected. Never yet had a sacked kitten or pup escaped him or hurt him even slightly.

He pulled out the half-dead gray kitten, killed it and laid it aside. The second gray kitten fought, but not very long or very hard. Then, suddenly, what the coyote knew as an old story took on a new and astonishing twist.

Instead of waiting to be pulled out of the sack, Frosty sprang out. Straight to the coyote's head he went, all four paws raking, while baby teeth found a mark. He could work no serious damage, but fighting on his side was a powerful ally whose presence Frosty did not even suspect.

The coyote had opened numerous sacks and each time everything had happened in exactly the same way. Deciding to his own satisfaction that they'd always continue to fall into the same pattern, he had prepared himself for nothing else. Frosty's vicious attack startled him, so that he leaped suddenly backwards. When he did, Frosty relinquished his hold and sprang away. But he did not do so aimlessly.

The coyote's backward leap brought him near the end of the rotting log and Frosty's night-piercing eyes found the hollow there. His feline brain, able to execute a plan the instant it was conceived, did the rest. The end of Frosty's tail disappeared into the hollow a half-inch ahead of the coyote's snapping jaws. Though the hollow was scarcely big enough to admit his small body, Frosty managed to turn around in it.

Three feet away, the coyote bent his head to peer into the hollow and his disappointed panting sounded in jerky sequence. Growling a warning, Frosty took no further action. This was as simple and precise as a mathematical formula. The coyote could kill him. The coyote wanted to kill him. But the kitten was in the hollow log and the coyote was not. If the coyote could get in, he'd be here. All these indisputable elements added up to the fact that, at least temporarily, Frosty was safe.

He crouched watchfully, not afraid of the coyote but not foolish enough to engage in a battle that he did not have to fight. He was no match for the creature, he knew it, and since there didn't seem to be anything he could do right now, he did nothing.

After a moment, the coyote went away. No fool, he was perfectly aware of the fact that he might growl and scratch at the hole all night and still not reach the black kitten. He paused long enough to eat the two gray kittens and padded away on silent paws.

Frosty stayed where he was for another twenty minutes. When he finally moved, he went only to the entrance of the hollow and lingered there for five minutes more. He thought the coyote had gone but he wanted to be sure, and only when he was sure did he drop out of the hollow onto the ground.

He went into a half-crouch, tail curled against his flank and tense muscles ready to carry him wherever circumstance indicated he should go. This was a wholly unfamiliar world, one in which he'd have to feel every inch of his way. The least wrong move could bring disaster. Finally, eyes and ears alert, he moved softly as a shadow.

Frosty paused beside the limp gunny sack. He touched it with an extended nose, then glided cautiously around it. There was nothing to indicate that the sack was dangerous, but it had trapped him once and might again. Save for scent that still lingered on the sack, there was nothing whatever to indicate that the two gray kittens had ever been.

Knowing that he must do something, but with no clear idea of what that might be or where he should go, Frosty started into the night. He halted suddenly, warned more by deep-seated instinct than anything he could see or hear, and stood quietly under a bush. A moment later, he saw a big bird, a cruising great horned owl, pass overhead. Frosty stayed where he was for ten minutes. He knew only that he must be cautious. He could not know that the owl was hunting, and that a tender young kitten would be as acceptable as anything else.

A half-hour later, Frosty came to a streamlet, one of many that pursued their winding courses across the mountain, tumbled down it and finally poured their waters into a river. He crouched full-length and lapped water with a dainty pink tongue. . . . The kitten licked his chops, waited a bit, then drank again.

His thirst satisfied, he attended to every cat's implicit

duty. Sitting down, he washed himself thoroughly with his tongue and used his front paws to groom that part of his fur which his tongue would not reach.

He licked his chops once more, smoothed his whiskers and wandered on. He struck at and missed a mouse that rustled the grass in front of him and watched, wide-eyed with wonder, when a rabbit bounded away. He missed another mouse and fluffed his fur and spat when a hunting fox rippled past.

Dawn found him in a grassy meadow. Little tendrils of moisture curled upward from dew-wet grass and a thin blanket of mist overhung the meadow. When something moved sluggishly in front of him, Frosty sprang to pin it down. His prize was a fat grasshopper, too torpid with morning cold to move swiftly. The kitten's tail lashed back and forth. He looked intently at this, the first catch he had ever made. Then he ate it and found it good.

Casting back and forth across the meadow, Frosty caught and ate grasshoppers until his stomach would hold no more.

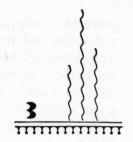

THE FIRST PLANTING

Strapped on a pack board borrowed from the express agent, the six crates were neither a heavy nor a clumsy burden. Each box was divided by a partition, with a muskrat at either end. Andy had specified that they be shipped in such a fashion because he wanted to be sure of mated pairs and he also wanted to be certain of forestalling domestic arguments among his charges. It was entirely possible that a male and female muskrat, regardless of how long they'd been mated, might start exercising their formidable cutting teeth on each other if put together in the same small crate. Now and again, there came a scraping of claws as one of the muskrats, unbalanced by a twist or turn, slid across the wooden floor of its prison.

As he carried his new acquisitions up the dark mountain, Andy pondered.

Muskrats, his research had taught him, are almost entirely aquatic creatures, though occasionally they make overland

29

journeys. Their food consists of aquatic plants, tender roots
and bulbs, and they are very fond of fresh-water mussels.
They construct houses of mud mixed with plant stalks or
dig burrows in the bank. The entrance to either type of
dwelling is always under water. They store food but remain
active under the ice all winter long.

Very prolific, they produce from two to five litters a year,
with from four to as many as a dozen young in each litter.
There is a reason for this. Muskrats, like rabbits, are the
prey of numerous things that walk, crawl or fly. They
counterbalance heavy casualties with large and frequent
families. Some naturalists claim that, by the end of the first
summer, the earliest young born will rear families of their
own. Others declare that no young breed until the spring
following their birth.

Because this was at best an uncertain experiment and
Andy could have no idea as to how it would work out, he
had chosen six mated pairs. His plan was to release them in
six different parts of the swamp and see where they flourished
best. After he had a better idea of what he was doing, he
could buy more breeding stock—but there was still one great
worry.

These muskrats had been reared in a large pond where,
insofar as they had had to find their own food, build their
own houses and dig their own burrows and tunnels, conditions were approximately the same as would have been
encountered in the wilderness. However, it was a fenced
pond and a carefully patrolled one. There had been no
predators to keep them alert, whereas the swamp was filled
with sudden death in many forms. Would pen-raised muskrats be able to survive the unfamiliar perils?

Andy carried his captives into the house, unbuckled the

straps that held their pens on his shoulders and eased them gently to the floor. He then separated the crates so that there was space between them. The animals emitted an offensive odor, but this was only because they had been in the tiny boxes so long. They'd cleanse themselves after they had room in which to do it. Unless they are sick, few animals will tolerate uncleanliness.

Andy grimaced. It was less than an alluring prospect to have the muskrats in his house all night, and, other things being equal, they'd be perfectly all right on the porch. But the battle had already started. If they were left outside, a prowling mink might well happen along and put an end to all twelve. It was wiser to endure the odor overnight and keep his charges safe.

Andy slept well, nevertheless. He was up and had breakfasted with the first hint of dawn. Kicking off his slippers, he pulled rubber boots over his trousers. The sun was just rising when, with five crates of muskrats back on the pack board—the sixth he intended to release in the watery slough directly in front of his house—he started out.

His step was light and his heart happy, as it always was when he went into the swamp. It was to Andy what his mountains are to the born mountaineer; his rolling prairie to the confirmed plainsman; his sun-scorched hills and forbidding acres of cactus to the desert lover. The swamp was grim and Andy knew it. But it was also beautiful and he saw its beauty. As no other place could ever be, it was home.

He wended his way around the watery slough. Swamp grasses, each one of which bore myriad seeds as delicate as fairy dust, brushed against him as he walked. Beneath his feet, the earth trembled. There were firm areas in the swamp, rocky places and high knolls where the green trees grew.

But much of that which was not given over to surface water was a huge, floating island, undermined by water. In numerous places, it was possible to stand on grass, punch a hole through to the water below, lower a baited hook and pull out a wriggling perch.

Andy walked swiftly and confidently, for he knew exactly where he was going. When he came to a long slough that varied between a foot and five feet in depth, he plunged unhesitatingly in and waded across without a thought for the death that lurked on either side. This was Dead Man's Slough. Across the center, where Andy had walked, extended a solid path which at no point was more than twenty inches wide. To step off that was to step into bottomless quicksand.

According to legend, an armed party of Trulls and Casmans, in close pursuit of Bije Gates, had turned back at Dead Man's Slough. Leading, Arvin Casman had stepped off the path and disappeared before his friends could help him. His bones were still in the quicksand. Andy didn't know and he didn't much care whether this tale was true. The feud was long over, a thing of the past, and sleeping dogs were better left alone. But it was a foregone conclusion that, if Arvin Casman or anyone else had stepped into Dead Man's Slough, his bones were still there.

At the far side of the slough, Andy turned left along its weed-lined shore, lowered his load to the ground, gently unfastened the wire that fastened one of the partitions shut and opened the door. A cautious brown nose was thrust forth and immediately withdrawn. The muskrat in the partition crouched nervously. Now and again there came the sound of a scraping paw.

Puzzled, Andy frowned. Then suddenly he understood. He had assumed that, after their long imprisonment in the tiny cages, the animals would be wild for freedom. However, they had been uprooted from safe and comfortable homes, endured a long and nerve-wracking journey, seen sights and heard sounds that must have been terrifying, and, through all this, they had stayed safe in their cages. It was small wonder that they were reluctant to leave. Andy tilted the box and spilled both its occupants into the water.

They went down, came up gasping and, for a short space, swam in a frenzied, meaningless fashion. Then their sudden fright passed. The nightmare was behind them. They were back in the water and muskrats are born for water. They began to enjoy themselves.

For the sheer luxury of so doing, they dived. Though they must have come within a hair's breadth of the bottom, they were such expert swimmers that they dislodged not even one fleck of mud. Forty feet away, they surfaced and played with each other for a moment. Somewhat clumsy on land, but incredibly graceful in the water, they swam around and around in the slough and regarded Andy with beady little black eyes.

Andy worried, for this was what he had feared most. Animals acquainted with danger would never expose themselves so recklessly. He threw pebbles at them, but though they dived when the pebbles splashed near, they surfaced again almost at once. Finally they swam to the weed-grown bank and began to eat ravenously.

Andy left them and went on. Throwing pebbles at this freshly liberated pair all day long, or all week long, would teach them nothing except how to dodge pebbles. If they were to survive in the swamp, they'd have to do so through their own instincts and intelligence, plus, probably, a great deal of luck.

Andy released his remaining pairs of muskrats at scattered points and returned the way he had come, to pick up the empty crates. Without so much as a glance for him, four of the five pairs he had freed were calmly eating the tender young shoots of marsh weeds or digging in the mud for bulbs. The remaining pair, the second he had liberated, dived hastily beneath an overhanging bank and refused to show themselves again. Andy began to have hopes. Perhaps it would not take the animals as long as he had thought it would to learn caution. Or maybe this pair was just naturally cautious. If they were, and remained that way, they stood a good chance of surviving.

Reaching home, Andy took his sixth and final pair of muskrats down to the watery slough in front of his house. He had deliberately saved them until last because he wanted to study at some length just how they reacted when released and just what they did.

Andy carried the crate to the water's edge, opened the door and jumped just in time. The first five pairs had huddled in their crates until spilled out, but these two had both ideas of their own and a grudge against the human race. As soon as the crate was opened, the two rushed Andy. Bristled, clicking their teeth, they pursued him for five yards. Then, as though discussing the situation between themselves, they clicked their teeth at each other and, in no hurry at all, turned back to the slough.

Andy grinned his appreciation. Together, the two muskrats weighed perhaps five pounds. He weighed a hundred and seventy. But they hadn't hesitated to charge him when they thought circumstances warranted it; there was nothing wrong with their courage. Andy watched them closely.

Still unhurried, and obviously with no intention of hurrying, the pair waddled back to the crate and inspected it thoroughly. Then they went into the water and their delight knew no bounds. They dived. Surfacing, they swam about for the sheer joy of swimming, then dived again. For a few minutes they occupied themselves eating swamp growth. Then they submerged beneath an embankment and a cloud of mud stained the water. Evidently this pair intended to lose no time in setting up housekeeping; the cloud of mud could mean only that they were excavating a burrow. The underwater entrance would lead upward into the bank.

One of the pair—it was hard to distinguish between them but Andy thought it was the male—came up for a hasty look around and promptly dived again. Muddy water continued to flow out from beneath the bank. Andy went to his house for a bite of lunch and when he returned to the slough the muskrats were still submerged. He grinned smugly. Obviously this particular pair of muskrats needed a den in a hurry and there could be only one reason for such a rush. A family was already on its way.

There was motion on the opposite side of the slough and a lithe brown mink appeared in the rushes there. It stood still, one paw raised like a pointing dog's and serpent-like head extended. After a moment, it slithered back into the rushes and disappeared. Andy frowned.

Mink are savage creatures, and now this one knew of the muskrats' presence. It had made no effort to investigate closely, either because it had just fed and wasn't hungry or because it had other game in mind. But it might have marked the muskrats as a possible future dinner and mink were almost the only predator able to follow a muskrat into its den.

Though they preferred peace, muskrats could fight savagely and they had the courage to fight. If there were easier game available, a mink might very well choose it rather than risk a battle. But a hunger-driven mink would never reckon the odds and unless it was very lucky, no muskrat could defeat or escape from one.

This presented a serious problem. Furs provided an important part of Andy's income. If he trapped the mink now, instead of waiting for cold weather to bring prime furs, he'd get nothing for it. But if the mink started killing his muskrats, he'd have to trap it. Mink were one of the many things he'd have to watch closely.

Late in the afternoon, Andy started back into the swamp to see how his charges were doing.

The pair he'd left in Dead Man's Slough were busy making themselves a house. When Andy approached, they swam cautiously to a clump of reeds and lurked near them. Studying him with watchful eyes, they swam in little circles. When he made a sudden move, they dived. Satisfied, Andy went on. These two were at least beginning to suspect that all callers wouldn't necessarily be friendly.

The second pair, the naturally cautious ones, were not in sight when Andy approached the slough where he'd left them. But dimly beneath the water he saw the entrance to a den. No doubt the muskrats were in it.

Andy came to the third slough just in time to see a clean-limbed gray fox, a muskrat dangling limply from his jaws, trotting away from it. Andy muttered under his breath. He hadn't brought a gun because, though he'd known that predators might be raiding his muskrats, he hadn't expected to catch any in the act. But from now on he must always be armed and definitely he would have to eliminate this particular fox. Having learned that it could catch muskrats, it might hunt them constantly and conceivably could catch all twelve.

Returning to his house, Andy took two fox traps and a bottle of fox scent from his storage room. Slipping the bottle into his pocket and taking the traps in one hand and his repeating .22 rifle in the other, he went back to the slough. He tied a flat stone to the pan of each trap, waded into the slough and set the traps so that only the stone protruded above water. Then he cut two willow withes and dipped one end of each into his bottle of fox scent. Eighteen inches from his traps, he thrust them into the mud until only the scented ends protruded. It was an old and effective trapper's trick, based on a fox's dislike of getting wet. Excited by the tantalizing scent and wanting to get close to it, the fox would use the stone on the trap pan as an effective means of so doing and, of course, spring the trap.

Twilight fell, and, in the gathering gloom of early evening, Andy hurried to the next slough. He halted in his tracks and muttered angrily. On a patch of smooth grass, five feet from the water's edge, lay the gnawed head and naked, scaley tail of a muskrat. There was no track or sign to show what had caught it, but clinging to a nearby reed, Andy found a cottony puff of fur from a bobcat. He muttered again.

It was too dark to go to the house for more traps, but it would be well to have some waiting here. The killer, probably a bobcat, knew of the other muskrat and would return to get it.

Andy trotted toward the next and last slough and found both muskrats swimming placidly. A split second later, a great horned owl dipped out of the sky, plucked one of the swimming animals from the water and floated away with its victim in its talons.

It happened so suddenly and so unexpectedly that Andy needed a moment to realize it had happened at all. It was like watching a peaceful scene in which a bomb is suddenly exploded. Uncannily silent wings giving not the slightest hint of his approach, the owl was not there, then he was, then he was gone. So perfectly timed and executed was the maneuver that it was carried through from start to finish without the owl's ruffling a single feather or missing one beat of his wings. It was a master feat by a master craftsman.

Leveling his rifle, sighting as best he could in the uncertain light, Andy snapped a shot after the fleeing owl. He shot a second time, a third, and watched the bird fly out of sight. When he lowered the rifle, there was dread in his heart.

He had hoped that, in time, his muskrats would come to know and learn to avoid land prowlers, such as foxes and bobcats. But there was not and couldn't possibly be any defense against raiding great horned owls. The wariest muskrat would never hear them coming and, nine times out of ten, would never see them. They were destruction itself, death in its most efficient form. A very few of them, hunting the swamp regularly, could make it impossible ever to raise muskrats there.

Andy made up his mind. No believer in the unnecessary destruction of anything at all, he must defend that which was his. The only possible course lay in keeping the swamp as free of great horned owls as he could.

Somewhat dejectedly, he made his way back to the house. Turning his swamp into a muskrat farm had seemed like a grand dream, but maybe it could never be anything except a dream. He had expected to lose some, but the first day was not yet ended and he'd lost a quarter of all the muskrats

liberated. If casualties kept up at this rate, he'd have none
left in another three days.

The next morning, carrying more traps and armed with
his .22, he went back into the swamp. Passing Dead Man's
Slough, he sighed in relief to discover that the two muskrats
he had left there were safe. The second pair, the cautious
ones, were not in sight but a partly finished house was evidence that they were still in the slough. Why they wanted a
house when they already had a den was puzzling, but Andy
supposed they had their own reasons.

Approaching the third slough, the one from which the
fox had taken the muskrat, Andy halted and stood quietly.

A leaning log angled from the bank into the slough, and
the surviving muskrat sat on it, shucking a fresh-water mussel.
It bit through the tough mechanism that clamped the shell,
scooped out and ate the tender flesh within, let the shell fall
into the water and dived for another mussel.

The gray fox that had caught the first muskrat had come
back for the second one. He was lying motionless on the
bank. As soon as the muskrat dived, the fox rose, paced
forward and, a split second before the muskrat's head broke
water, went into another crouch.

Slowly, making no swift move that would call attention
to himself, Andy raised and sighted his rifle. But he did not
shoot because he was interested.

The fox, evidently a young one that had not yet learned
that it pays to look in all directions all the time, was so intent
on the muskrat that it paid no attention to anything else.
The muskrat climbed out on the log, ate his mussel and
dived for another one. The fox rose, paced forward, and
threw himself down again.

Crouching, he seemed a part of the grass and Andy could

not help admiring both his plan and the way he was putting it into effect. He continued to hold his fire because here was a chance to learn exactly how foxes catch muskrats and such knowledge might very well be useful. The muskrat reappeared, climbed on the log . . . and the fox leaped.

He should have pinned his quarry, but something warned the muskrat and the fox was still in the air when it rolled off the log and dived. Struggling wildly, the fox splashed water with his front paws and fought desperately to get back onto the bank. He could not.

The bottom of this slough was stony for the most part, but just off the bank from which the fox had leaped was more quicksand and the animal was hopelessly enmeshed in it. He made a mighty effort to hold his nose out of water and Andy's shot caught him in the head just before he went down. It was by far the kindest thing to do.

Andy was surprised and pleased when the day passed and he lost no more muskrats. He was mystified when a whole week went by with no further losses. Then the answer occurred to him. Muskrats, like everything else, produce their quota of fools, and two of the three that had died the first day probably belonged in that category. The third, the one taken by the great horned owl, had been just plain unlucky.

Andy caught a young bobcat, picked up his traps . . . and in three days lost the two muskrats in Dead Man's Slough and the one whose mate had been killed by the bobcat! There were neither tracks nor any other sign to identify the raider, but on one of the high knobs Andy found him.

It was another great horned owl that sat quietly in a gnarled oak, with his tufted ears silhouetted against the sky and his eyes closed against the sun's glare. Andy's shot caught him squarely, and he flapped his wings just once as he toppled from the perch.

Leaving him where he fell, Andy went ruefully home. It was very evident that muskrat farming was somewhat less than the ideal way to get rich quick. Of his original stock of twelve, he had exactly six left. They were the pair in front of his house, the cautious pair, and two singles. Not too much could be expected from them, and Andy thought of his lean bank balance. To buy more muskrats for predators to kill fell short of wise investment.

Dejectedly Andy went to the slough in front of his house and sat with his arms clasping his knees. The male muskrat came up to stare haughtily at him and Andy stared defiantly back.

"All right!" he invited. "Go ahead and look!"

The muskrat—Andy had whimsically named the pair Four-Leaf and Clover—made a lazy circle and turned to fix unblinking eyes on the boy. Andy grimaced. At no time had he exerted the slightest effort to make pets of any of his charges because it was better to have them wild. But Four-Leaf and Clover, living so near and visited so frequently, were on familiar terms with him. He had an uncomfortable feeling that they were not on equal terms. Four-Leaf and Clover considered themselves vastly superior to any mere human being!

"If you don't wipe that sneer off your face," Andy threatened, "I'll turn you into a genuine muskrat-hide glove!"

He picked up a pebble and was about to plunk it into the water near Four-Leaf when Clover's head broke water. Behind her, in formation so precise that they seemed to have drilled for it, came an even dozen small copies of herself. Andy dropped the pebble and a broad smile lighted his face.

"Glory be! Darned if we'uns haven't got ourselves some babies!"

His dejection melted like mist before the rising sun. Happily he pulled on his boots and went into the swamp. He'd lost half his original stock and still had six more muskrats than he'd started with. Reaching the slough where the cautious pair lived, Andy crouched quietly in the grass beside it.

A half hour later, they appeared with ten babies, and when Andy passed the sloughs inhabited by lone muskrats whose mates had been killed, he was amazed to find each of them with eight young. Obviously, both females had survived.

Jubilantly, Andy threw his hat into the air, and when he reached home he went carefully over his plans for the future. If he forgot about the new rifle he had intended to give himself for Christmas and made his old clothes last a while longer, he could buy twenty more mated pairs. The next morning he walked into town and mailed his order.

A week later, while patrolling the swamp to inspect his various colonies of muskrats, Andy saw a great horned owl flying low over the grass with what appeared to be a black muskrat in its talons. Suddenly the victim twisted about to attack its captor.

When they came nearer, Andy saw, to his vast astonishment, that the supposed muskrat was a black kitten!

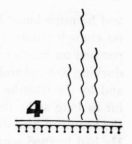

4

FEATHERED DEATH

His stomach filled with grasshoppers, Frosty went to one of several large pine stumps that were spotted here and there about the meadow and crawled beneath an out-jutting root, from the under side of which the earth had crumbled away. He lay perfectly still and went to sleep.

Aside from Luke Trull and the coyote, he knew nothing of the enemies he might find in these wild uplands. However, there were sure to be some, and certainly he would be much harder to find beneath the root than he would if he merely lay down on some grassy bed. But he was incapable of sodden slumber.

A part of him that never slept was aware of wind rippling the grass; the furtive rustlings and scrapings of a family of mice that dwelt in a tiny burrow beneath the same root; the chattering of a blue jay that, having nothing to scold, was scolding anyhow. Frosty eased into wakefulness.

He knew the wind and he knew the mice, but not the jay

45

and he must know it. Without seeming to move, he edged far enough around the root so he could see the bird. It was perched on another stump, flitting its wings, flicking its tail, ducking its head and scolding. Frosty studied it for a second, and by the time he went back to sleep it was assured that, for as long as he lived, he would associate the sound with the beautiful bird that made it and the bird with the sound. He had learned something else. Never again, if he heard a blue jay screech, would he have to waken and look for it.

He thought of the shed from which Luke Trull had taken him, but not with any feeling of nostalgia or homesickness because the shed belonged to yesterday. That was there and he was here, and even if he wished to do so, he would be unable to find it again. Nor, aside from the fact that he wanted to stay in or very near the meadow, did he have any plans.

A rover by nature, he must not rove until conditions were much more auspicious than they were right now. What he knew about the hills consisted largely of the fact that he did not know them at all. But if he stayed near the meadow, he was certain of finding plenty of fat grasshoppers to eat any time he was hungry. It was a common sense decision.

When five deer came slowly into the meadow, Frosty's built-in ear antenna immediately picked up the thudding of their hooves and a moment later he heard their noisy chewing as they ate grass. He stayed where he was, lacking the slightest idea as to what manner of creature had come into the meadow now but determined to find out. They were feeding toward his stump.

Twenty minutes later, they were directly in front of it and, as before, Frosty eased just far enough out so he could see them. They were big animals, but obviously they in-

tended no harm. When the shuffling hooves of one disturbed
a meadow mouse that leaped in wild panic toward the stump,
Frosty had only to move aside in order to catch it. He
pinned the mouse with his paws, ended its tiny struggle with
his teeth and gazed defiantly at the deer.

They swung their heads toward him, jaws moving in grace-
less discord as they continued to chew the grass with which
they had filled them. Then they lowered their heads to crop
more grass.

Frosty lay down to eat his prize, liking the taste of hot
flesh in his mouth and the salty tang of fresh-caught prey.
He ate all except the hairless tail, and the mouse whetted
his appetite for more. Slipping out from beneath his root,
he looked about for the deer.

Still cropping gustily, they were feeding toward the forest
on the far side of the meadow. Frosty minced after them.
They had driven one mouse from its covert; the chances
were that they would drive more. Frosty edged up to a sleek
doe that suddenly wheeled and pounded down on him.

Just in time, he saved himself by slipping behind a
boulder. . . . When he could no longer hear the plunging
doe, he peered over it. She had resumed feeding. More
watchful now, Frosty slunk toward the deer. They saw him
but paid no attention. Evidently they did not mind his
trailing them. They did not want him on the place where
they were feeding now or where they might feed a moment
from now.

Another mouse panicked. Frosty caught and ate it. By
the time he had a third mouse, his appetite was satisfied. In
addition, he had learned a priceless lesson; large grazing
beasts are apt to disturb small creatures that dwell in the
grass. The deer, having grazed their fill, drifted to beds in

the shady forest. Frosty curled up in a sunny spot and let this new world come to him.

When two more crows winged lazily over the meadow, cawing as they flew, he knew it as the same sound he had heard while a prisoner in the sack and satisfied his curiosity on that score. He was alert to every furtive rustling, every note in the multi-toned song the breeze sang, every motion in the grass and every flutter of every leaf on a grove of nearby sycamores.

The creatures that lived in the meadow were small ones; various insects; moles and mice; cottontail rabbits and harmless snakes. Frosty identified each in turn and after he'd done so, he stored each away in his brain. Having met and known anything at all, it was his forever. He'd never forget it and never fail to know it should he meet it again. But there was much that he did not know and the unknown roused his instant curiosity. When he saw a flicker of motion over near the sycamores, he concentrated his whole attention on it.

He did not know that he'd seen one of two gray squirrels that had chosen to abide for a couple of days in the sycamores, or that all he'd seen was a glimpse of its tail as it climbed a tree. It was strange and he could not rest until it was familiar. Frosty began to stalk the sycamores, and the stalk saved his life.

He saw nothing and heard nothing, but the same coyote that had ripped the sack open was suddenly upon him. Knowing of the gray squirrels, and hoping to catch one or the other on the ground, the coyote had been stalking the sycamores, too. Finding Frosty, the creature had accepted him instead.

Not stopping to see what threatened, but reacting instantly, Frosty sprang for a sycamore trunk and drew himself up less than two inches ahead of the coyote's snapping jaws. He climbed to the sycamore's crotch and turned to look down. Tongue lolling like a dog's, the coyote looked anxiously up and whined his disappointment. Then, realizing he'd get nothing among the sycamores, he turned away to hunt some rabbits with whose thicket he was acquainted.

Frosty remained in the sycamore's crotch. Though he had considered himself very alert, he'd had no slight inkling of the coyote's presence until it was almost too late. Concentrating on the gray squirrel, he had given little thought to the fact that something might be stalking him. Never again must he be so lax—but he had learned.

Had he been beneath the root, very probably the coyote might have dug him out. But, as had just been proven, the coyote was unable to climb trees. It followed, therefore, that a tree would be a much safer place in which to rest. Frosty cleaned his fur, and when one of the gray squirrels appeared in the higher branches of the same tree, he looked at it with challenging interest. But the squirrel fled in panic-stricken terror when it saw the kitten.

Frosty stayed in his perch until just before nightfall, then descended to hunt again. But the grasshoppers, that had been so easy to catch when numbed by early morning cold, were amazingly agile now. The kitten stalked one that was crawling up a blade of grass. Escaping from between his clutching claws, the insect spread bright-colored wings and flew away. Frosty marked it down, but when he went to the place where it had descended, it was not there. Alighting, the grasshopper had crawled along the ground. Presently, four feet to one side, it spread gaudy wings and took flight once more.

Again Frosty marked it down and again failed to find it.

Crawling beneath a dead weed that matched its drab color exactly, the grasshopper was remaining perfectly still.

An hour's hard hunting brought the black kitten one grasshopper, a vast frustration and a mounting hunger. Then twilight crept stealthily over the hills and the grasshoppers settled down in various places where they would pass the hours of darkness. Because they did not move at all and were almost perfectly camouflaged when holding still, and because it was dark, Frosty could not see them.

He pounced eagerly when a mouse rustled in front of him. But since he did not know how to hunt mice—the only ones he'd caught were those that fled in terror from the feeding deer—he missed. He ambled disconsolately down to the cold little stream that wandered through the meadow.

He was hungry and growing hungrier, but he had not forgotten the earlier lesson of the day when, because he'd given all his attention to the gray squirrel in the sycamores, the coyote had almost caught him. Though he was principally interested in getting anything at all to eat, he did not neglect that which lay about him. When he came near the stream, he knew that something else was already there. He stalked cautiously forward until he could see what it was.

A mink crouched on the stream bank, busily eating a fourteen-inch trout that it had surprised in the shallows. Sure of its own powers, fearing nothing, the mink gave no attention to anything save the meal it had caught. Finished, it licked its chops and turned to stare at the tall grass in which Frosty lay.

The mink knew and had known since the kitten came that Frosty was there, for its nose had told it. A bloody little creature, ordinarily it might have amused itself by killing the kitten. But a full belly can make even a mink feel good, and after a moment, it turned to travel down-stream.

Frosty stole forward to find the trout's tail, head and fins. The epicurean mink had chosen only the choice portions and left this carrion for any scavenger that might come. But it was good and it dulled Frosty's hunger. His meal ended, he washed up, then and went back into the meadow.

No longer hungry and thus no longer finding it necessary to devote his attention to finding food, the kitten could concentrate on the other creatures that had come into the meadow. He sat on a hillock to watch a fox hunt mice.

It was a big, sleek dog fox, with a mate and cubs back in a hillside den, and it made not the slightest effort to stalk its quarry. Instead, it walked openly, head up and ears alert. When it heard a mouse in a grass-thatched runway, the fox reared, to come stiffly down with both front paws. Five times it reared, and five times it pinned the mouse it wanted and extricated it from the grass beneath which it was pinned.

Suddenly the fox smelled Frosty and whirled. It came trotting, its attitude more one of aroused curiosity than hostility. The kitten was something new, and before the fox took any further action, it wanted to know exactly what this strange creature was. Its head curving gracefully toward Frosty, it stopped four feet away.

Trapped and knowing it, the kitten made ready to fight. He laid his ears back and framed a snarl on his jaws. The growl that rumbled from his chest was the most ferocious of which he was capable. Looking more amused than cautious, the fox extended an exploring paw. Frosty struck and missed. He was no match for this veteran of the wilderness. The fox circled and the kitten turned with him.

After a short space, seemingly well-entertained, the fox

padded away. No wanton killer, it was a good hunter and, in this time of plenty, it could take its choice of mice, fat rabbits, or plump grouse. Any one of them was preferable to this snarling kitten, though had it been lean hunting, or had the fox been hungry enough, Frosty would have died right there.

The black kitten tried to hunt mice as he had seen the fox catch them, but, though he could hear them scurrying along their runways, his timing was poor and his knowledge scant. One needed the skill that only experience brought to succeed at this sort of hunting. Frosty leaped a dozen times without pinning even one mouse.

When the five deer came back into the meadow, he trotted eagerly toward them. Though they had no war with mice, the deer never cared where they walked. Their hooves penetrated grass-roofed runways and now and then plowed into a nest. Whenever they did, the mice suffered a panic that momentarily robbed them of reason or of any desire save to escape destruction.

The feeding deer disturbed two that Frosty caught and ate. With the first light of morning, hunger satisfied, he returned to his sycamore and climbed to the familiar crotch. Impatiently he lay down. He was fed and tired, and he wanted to sleep, but the cold morning wind ruffled his fur and made comfortable sleep impossible.

Any other animal would have accepted conditions as they were and slept anyhow. Frosty was a cat, and cats never accept second best if they can get the best.

Frosty climbed out on one of the sycamore's massive limbs until the slender branches in which the limb terminated swayed beneath his weight. That made him afraid of falling, so he turned and went back. But he was still disinclined to accept a bed where the cold wind could chill him if there were a possibility of something better. He tried a second limb, a third, then went up the trunk and found exactly what he sought.

A big limb, growing out of the trunk, had rotted and fallen. In falling, it had left a cavity that had been enlarged by a pair of pileated woodpeckers which had nested in it over a period of years. Blowing leaves had sifted in and partly filled the hollow, and the cold wind seethed harmlessly past. Frosty found it a warm, dry and safe bed. Since the opening was barely big enough to admit him, he could defend it against anything else that tried to enter.

More than once, in the days that followed, it was necessary for him to fill his belly with grasshoppers only for the simple reason that he could catch nothing else. He learned to see them in the grass, and to gauge his strike so he could catch them before they were able to take to the air. He became an expert hunter of grasshoppers, and the precise training this afforded helped him in other ways.

The mice in their grass-thatched runways could never be seen. They must be heard, and since the strike was always blind, it had to be exact. A fraction of an inch one way or the other and the mouse escaped. Frosty learned to strike so expertly that almost never did his victim elude him. Only when he was feeling lazy or had a run of bad luck did he depend on the browsing deer to flush his mice for him.

As he lived, so did he learn. Stealthy footsteps foretold some slinking beast of prey. But so did the sudden chatter of an excited bird, a madly-scooting rabbit, or the deer when they stopped eating and became alert. Frosty taught himself to read such signs, and by them he always knew when the coyote or some other dangerous creature was aprowl. He acquired a vast confidence in his own ability to meet and overcome any dangers that threatened.

Hunting mice in the meadow one night, he came face to face with a bobcat that was similarly engaged. The bobcat snarled and leaped at him, and had he turned to run, Frosty would have been overtaken and killed. Instead of running, he stood his ground and spat back. The bobcat, pretending vast interest in a clump of grass near the kitten, scraped the grass with contemptuous feet and stalked away.

Frosty extended his range from the meadow into the woods, and each journey became a bit longer and a bit more daring. He not only lived but lived well, and his first great triumph was achieved some six weeks after he came to the meadow.

Every afternoon, when the sun was hot and high, a mother grouse led her five bobtailed young to some abandoned ant hills beside the forest. The birds burrowed luxuriously in the gritty earth, working it into their feathers and using their wings and beaks to throw it over their backs. The sand and grit acted as a cleansing bath.

Occasionally other predators visited the meadow in the afternoon, but the grouse came so quietly that these passers-by never knew of them. Frosty, who hunted the meadow almost every afternoon, knew all about them. But after stalking his stealthiest, only to have the mother grouse sound a warning and the whole brood take wing in his very face, he gave himself over to studying them. They were very difficult to stalk because the grass around the ant hills was short and he could be seen. But after two weeks, he thought he saw a way.

This afternoon, a full hour before the grouse family was due to come out of the woods, Frosty was lying motionless behind one of the ant hills. His eyes were unblinking and even the tip of his tail did not twitch. To all appearances, he was a dead thing.

He heard the grouse coming; they were announced by the tiny sounds of their own feet and the mother's querulous clucking as she warned her young to take every care. Frosty remained motionless until two of the young grouse mounted the very ant hill behind which he lay. Then, without seeming to move at all and certainly without visible effort, he was up and over. While the other grouse took thundering wing, he fastened his claws in one and pulled it down.

That gave him an inflated idea of his own prowess, and the next afternoon he was again hiding in the ant hills, waiting for the grouse. They did not come. The young were silly and inexperienced but the mother was no fool. She would never be deceived by the same ruse twice in succession. However, catching just one grouse gave Frosty so much confidence that he increased his field vastly, and as he did, he learned still more.

Because enemies could be anywhere, it was at all times necessary to be sharply alert. But Frosty had already discovered that the things besides himself which could climb trees were disinclined to be hostile, and, once in the forest, he was never very far from a convenient tree. He changed his sleeping place from the sycamore's hollow trunk to the hollow limb of a massive oak in the forest.

He also did more of his hunting in the forest. The place teemed with young rabbits and grouse, many of which were adventurous, incautious, downright silly, or a combination of all three. His kills consisted almost exclusively of these easy-to-catch creatures but, in catching the young and foolish, he was laying the groundwork that would later enable him to bring down the wise and experienced.

Frosty's move into the forest brought increased skill in hunting, but it also brought disaster.

He was prowling one morning when he heard, smelled and then saw a coyote coming. Deliberately, Frosty showed himself. This was a game he had learned to play, gauging exactly every move the coyote made. When his antagonist rushed, Frosty waited until the last possible second before scrambling up the slender trunk of a black birch. He halted just beyond reach of his enemy's strongest leap and looked down contemptuously.

Suddenly he was wrenched from the tree and suspended in mid air. He did not know what had happened, for he had seen and heard nothing, but he did know that he must not submit meekly to anything at all. He tried to twist himself and rise to attack whatever held him. Now he saw that it was a great bird.

Frosty had been plucked from his perch by a great horned owl, but he was lucky. Three days ago, in a foray against Ira Casman's chickens, the owl had been repelled by a shotgun in the hands of Ira's brother. Too fine to kill, the number ten shot had only wounded and weakened him. He had since missed every strike at everything and now, famished, he had caught the first creature he could that might be edible. However, instead of being deeply imbedded, his claws were hooked only through the loose skin on Frosty's back.

The owl winged toward a pine stub, alighted on a branch and turned to kill his captive so he could eat it. But the second he found a purchase for his feet, Frosty attacked furiously. He sank his teeth through feathers into flesh, even while he raked with his claws. Always before, such of the owl's victims as had lived until they were landed in a tree were terrified and shivering, easy prey. He had bargained for no such fury as this.

He took wing again, and this time his course led across the swamp. On the other side was a ledge of rock. Even a cat, dropped from any considerable height onto it, would not be likely to move again.

Frosty knew only that he was helpless, and the knowledge redoubled his anger. He twisted and turned, doing his best to fling himself into any position from which he could claw or bite his captor. Without knowing what it was or what it meant, he heard Andy Gates's shot.

He did know that the owl went suddenly limp and that they plummeted toward the swamp. Strikingly, Frosty was momentarily stunned. He tried dazedly to get up and run away when something else seized him.

He turned to attack this new enemy.

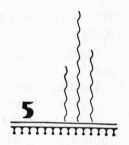

5

PARTNERS

Twisting himself almost double, Frosty sank his teeth into the fleshy part of Andy's hand and raked with all four paws. Blood welled from the scratches and cuts and dripped onto the dead owl. But instead of flinging the kitten from him, Andy encircled Frosty's neck with his right thumb and forefinger, rendered his front paws ineffective by slipping his other three fingers behind them, grabbed his rear paws with his left hand and stretched him out. He murmured,

"If you aren't the little spitfire!"

Unable to do anything else, Frosty could only glare. The smile that always lingered in Andy's eyes almost flashed to his lips. His face softened. He spoke soothingly,

"You might as well stop it. You'd have a real rough time clawing me all to bits."

Frosty snarled and Andy grinned. He'd never had a cat or thought of getting one, but besides his fighting heart, there was something about Frosty to which he warmed.

Without thinking that he too had defied conventional living, Andy recognized something akin to himself. He said firmly,

"You're going to get some help whether you want it or not."

Holding Frosty so that he could neither scratch nor bite, Andy carried him back to the house, pushed the door open with his knee and wondered. The kitten must be hurt because nothing withstood the strike of a great horned owl without getting hurt. In spite of the fact that he did not appear to be seriously injured, he probably would bear watching for a few days. Andy thought speculatively of one of the cages in which the muskrats had been shipped. He'd be able to watch the spunky little fellow closely if he put him in one.

For no apparent reason, he suddenly remembered when he had lived in town, working on the railroad nights and going to school days. There had always been a feeling of too little room and too much confinement. He looked again at Frosty . . . and put him down on the floor.

"Guess we won't lock you up."

Frosty scooted beneath the stove and again Andy's smile threatened to blossom. Running, the kitten looked oddly like a strip of black velvet upon which frost crystals sparkle. It was then that Andy gave him his name.

"Okeh, Frosty. If that's what you like, that's what you can have."

He stooped to peer beneath the stove and was warned away with a rumbling growl, so he straightened. After he had satisfied himself that the kitten was all right, Frosty would be free to go his own way. There never had been and never would be any prisoners in the swamp.

Going outside, careful to latch the door behind him lest

it blow open and let Frosty escape, Andy caught up a discarded tin can and took a spade from his shed. He turned
the rich muck at the swamp's edge, dropped the fat worms
he uncovered into the can, then went back to the house for
a willow pole with a line, hook and cork bobber attached.
Carrying the pole and can of worms, he made his way to
the watery slough in front of his house.

While their dozen children sported in the slough, Four-
Leaf and Clover dug succulent bulbs in the mud on the
opposite bank. None paid any attention to Andy. This
colony, protected by the nearness of the house and seeming
to know it, was not nearly as wary as those that lived in more
remote sections of the swamp. Even the great horned owls
had not attacked them. Andy strung a wriggling worm on
his hook and was about to cast it when,

"Howdy."

Andy turned to face Luke Trull, who had stolen upon him
unseen and unheard. Still wearing his sun-faded trousers
and torn shirt, still needing a haircut and shave, his eyes
were fixed on the muskrats in the slough. Andy's heart sank.
He'd feared the native swamp predators. But not even the
great horned owls could work the same fearful damage as
Luke Trull, should he decide to come raiding. Andy said
coldly,

"Hi, Luke."

"I heerd tell," the other smirked, " 'bout somethin' new
in the swamp."

"Who told you?"

"News gits 'round."

"There is something new. But it belongs to me and so
does the swamp. Both are to be left alone."

"Oh sure. Sure 'nough. I aim to leave 'em alone. They's mushrats, ain't they?"

"That's right. They're muskrats."

"Wu'th a heap of money, ain't they?"

"Not a 'heap.' Maybe a couple of dollars or so for a good prime pelt."

"Could be a heap given a man ketches enough of 'em. How many you got all told?"

"Not enough to start trapping."

"The hills is full of talk 'bout how you've turned your no-count swamp into a mushrat farm. They's talk 'bout how you aim to get rich off mushrat pelts."

"Nobody's going to get rich. And anybody who traps any muskrats before I give the word, or without my permission, will be in trouble."

"Oh, sure. Sure 'nough. But I've already said I don't aim to bother 'em none."

Andy said shortly, "That's a good idea. I'll be seeing you, Luke."

"Yep. I'll be 'round."

The lean hillman drifted away as silently as he had come and Andy cast his baited hook. But his thoughts were troubled ones.

He had hoped to keep his muskrat ranch a secret, but he should have known the impossibility of that. Only he knew all the safe paths through the swamp, but Luke Trull, the Haroldsons and the Casmans knew some of them. Frequently they came to fish in some favored slough or other. Somebody must have seen a colony of muskrats—perhaps they'd stumbled across Four-Leaf and Clover and their family—and it hadn't been hard to piece the rest of the story together. Probably Johnny Linger, the express agent, hadn't talked to any hillman. But Johnny had friends in town to whom he might have talked, his friends had friends, and by the time enough people knew the story, it could easily get back to the hill dwellers.

Andy was so absorbed with this new problem that he was entirely unaware of the fact that his cork bobber had disappeared. He yanked the pole, missed his strike and strung another worm on the stripped hook. He might post his swamp against trespassers. Not that trespass signs had ever kept a single Casman, Haroldson—or especially a Trull— from going where he wished to go but at the very least they'd be evidence that he had acted in his own behalf. But trespass signs or not, there was going to be trouble in plenty if human predators started raiding his muskrats and trouble was always better avoided.

He missed another nibble and began to concentrate on his fishing. Very possibly he was killing his ogres before he met them. But when Luke Trull saw a possibility of earning money without working for it—?

The bobber disappeared again. Andy struck in time, lifted a flapping jumbo perch out of the slough, put it on a stringer, rebaited and cast his line. There was little sport in catching the perch with such heavy tackle, but they were delicious eating and the slough swarmed with them. Andy fished until he had six.

He sat down, scaled his catch, ran his knife along each side of their backbones, and removed the tasty fillets. The offal, which ordinarily he would have thrown away, he laid on a saucer-sized lily pad and took to the house with him. Still beneath the stove, Frosty greeted him with a bubbling growl. Andy wrapped four of the fish heads in a piece of discarded newspaper and put them in his icebox. The remainder, along with the offal, he placed on a saucer and thrust beneath the stove. He remembered to put a dish of water beside the saucer.

Andy prepared a batch of biscuits, fried his own fish, ate lunch and washed the dishes. The untouched fish heads remained where he had placed them, and when he stooped to peer beneath the stove, Frosty glared back balefully. A little worried that the kitten might be hurt worse than he appeared to be, Andy closed and latched the door and took the trail to town. Uneasy feelings stirred within him.

The town, he had long ago decided to his own satisfaction, had little real touch with the hills. To the townspeople, the hillmen were a strange breed, like lions in a zoo, and as such they could always furnish entertainment. Regardless of the work, hopes and dreams it had taken to put them there, few townsmen could be expected to take seriously a swamp with muskrats in it. Stealing goods from a town store would be a criminal offense and provoke righteous indignation. Stealing muskrats from his swamp would be just another example of what the hillmen were always doing to each other and provoke, at the very most, a sympathetic chuckle.

Even as he walked resolutely ahead, Andy thought that he would have to stand alone. Nevertheless, he still felt he must try to enlist aid. An ounce of prevention was definitely worth at least a pound of cure, and though nothing had happened as yet, now was the time to take steps in his own defense. But what could he do and who would listen?

Reaching town, Andy turned aside to the State Police substation. The harassed-appearing trooper in charge put aside the report upon which he was working and looked up questioningly.

"My name's Gates," Andy introduced himself. "Andy Gates. I want to post my land against trespassers."

"Well—has someone tried to stop you?"

"No," Andy admitted, "but suppose I post it and someone trespasses? What's the penalty?"

The trooper traced a meaningless doodle with his pen. "That depends a lot on circumstances. Few judges or justices are inclined to be harsh with a person who merely walks on another's property, even if it is posted."

"Suppose they steal?"

"That's entirely different. What have they stolen?"

"Nothing yet."

"Well," the trooper's voice was edged with sarcasm, "what do you think they might steal?"

"Muskrats."

"Muskrats?" Puzzled wrinkles furrowed the trooper's brow. "Do you have some?"

"Yes."

"Are they penned?"

"No, they're running loose in my swamp."

"Then how can you claim they're yours?"

"I bought and paid for them and the swamp's private property."

"Well," the trooper shrugged, "when somebody starts stealing them, you come see us."

Andy turned dejectedly away. If it were a hoard of gold or jewels in his swamp, the trooper would have understood instantly and taken the proper steps to protect it. The boy grinned wryly. Doubtless the trooper thought he was a harmless crackpot and was even now congratulating himself on being rid of him so easily.

Andy went to see the official whom he had planned to

consult from the first. Joe Wilson, the district game warden, was old and would give way to a younger man soon, but he was wise in the ways of the hills and he knew the hillmen as few townspeople did. Andy came to his house, knocked and was admitted by Lois, the pleasant-faced daughter who kept house for Joe.

"Why hello, Andy. Goodness! It's been a while since we've seen you. Do come in."

"Is your dad home, Lois?"

"In his study. Go right in."

There was a pang in her voice, for there had been a time when no daylight hours, and frequently few night hours, would have found Joe Wilson behind his desk. Now, when he went into the hills at all, it was only to those places which could be reached by car. Lean as a weasel, the way he had spent his life was written in his seamed face and wise eyes. Storms and sun and wind had marked his face, age and experience had implanted the wisdom in his eyes. He swung on his worn swivel chair to face Andy.

"Hi, young feller."

"Hi, Joe." Andy shook the warden's extended hand. "You're looking great."

"I may be good for a few days yet. What's on your mind?"

"I need your advice."

"So?"

"I've stocked my swamp with muskrats and—"

Andy told of the six pairs of muskrats he had planted in his swamp. He spoke of their misadventures with the fox and bobcat and of raiding great horned owls. But in spite of losses, the survivors had produced thirty-eight young. They had not only adjusted themselves to the swamp but had learned how to protect their babies. Naturally, there would be some losses among the young, but, as far as Andy knew, there hadn't yet been any. He had ordered twenty more mated pairs, which were due next week. He knew he'd lose some, perhaps half or even more, but some would survive and multiply. Next spring, when muskrat pelts were at their best, he'd harvest a few, if conditions so warranted. If not enough muskrats survived the winter, he'd let them go another season or more. He hoped that, over the years, he might build up enough of a muskrat population so that harvesting the surplus every year would be profitable. However, he had no illusions of great wealth.

When he was finished, Joe Wilson tamped a blackened pipe full of tobacco, lighted it and puffed soberly for a moment. Then he turned to Andy.

"Seems to me you're doing all right by yourself. Why do you need my advice?"

"Luke Trull has found out about it."

"Oh, gosh!"

Andy said dryly, "I know what you mean."

"You leatherhead! Why didn't you take them in at night and plant them back in the swamp? You know places there that nobody else can reach."

"I did take them in at night, but I wanted to keep one pair under close observation, so I released them in the slough in front of my house. Somebody saw them, or somebody, fishing back in the swamp, stumbled across another colony. Then too, I think Johnny Linger talked. They came, of course, through his station."

"Johnny wouldn't talk."

"Not to Luke Trull," Andy conceded. "But he has friends in town. They have friends, and the news got around. What can I do?"

"Have you been to the State Police?"

"Yes. They told me to wait until somebody starts poaching, then come to them and they'd see what they could do about it."

"They can't do anything," Joe Wilson said quietly. "They'd have to catch Luke in the act, and knowing him as I do, they can't. I know that he's been violating game laws ever since he was old enough to shoot a gun or cast a line, but I myself have been able to catch him only once in fifteen years. You're in for trouble, Andy."

"I know it. Will posting the swamp help?"

"Will a trespass sign keep Luke Trull out of any place he wants to go into?"

"No."

"Nor will anything else. He's mean as a mink and crafty as a shot-stung mallard. He'll find a way to get into your back sloughs and eddys; a shallow-draft boat light enough to carry will take him there. He won't be stopped as long as he scents money in the offing."

Andy said grimly, "I could meet him, explain that he was to stay out of the swamp and back it up with fists."

"Do that and you're in trouble," Joe Wilson pointed out. "Luke wouldn't fight back. But he would gallop that horse of his all the way into town and swear out an assault warrant. It'd be you, not Luke, whom the State Police would bring in."

"If he was caught with muskrat pelts, wouldn't it be proof that he stole them from me?"

Joe Wilson shrugged. "There's two hundred miles of streams and fifty different ponds back in those hills, and the trapping season is open to anyone with a license. Luke could, and would, say he took his pelts elsewhere."

"There are no muskrats anywhere except in my swamp."

"Do you know every pond and every foot of stream?"

"Of course not."

"Then how would you expect to convince a judge or justice? One muskrat pelt looks exactly like another; there's nothing special to mark yours."

"Isn't there anything I can do?"

"Yes there is, Andy. Has it occurred to you that your muskrat ranch will either have to be something pretty decent or else not worth bothering with?"

"What do you mean?"

The warden shrugged. "Just this. Considering the price of muskrats, you'll have to have plenty of 'em to make the thing pay off. Their pelts are at the best in late winter and early spring. To make it worthwhile, you'll have to have a great many and you won't be able to handle 'em all anyhow. Now Ira and Jud Casman are decent enough people. So are Old Man Haroldson and his sons. Take them into your confidence. Ask them to lay off until you have a trapping stock, and promise that, when and if you get one, they can help you reap your harvest. You won't be able to do it all, anyhow. They'll understand and I'm sure they'll cooperate."

"They won't be able to keep Luke off my neck."

"Nobody," said Joe Wilson, "ever kept Luke off anybody's neck, once he has decided to land on it. Do you know what I'd do?"

"What?"

"Hope he falls in a quicksand slough, if he comes for your muskrats!" the warden said grimly. "Failing that, you'll just have to meet any situation as it arises. I wish you luck."

"Thanks," Andy murmured. "It looks as though I'll need it. Well, I'll be getting back."

"Stay and have a bite with us."

"I'd like to but I left a kitten that thinks he's a tiger under my kitchen stove. I'd better get back and make sure he hasn't clawed the house to bits. He looked as though he'd like to do just that."

The sun was sinking when Andy arrived home. A rattlesnake, sluggishly digesting a chipmunk it had caught, rattled a desultory warning without moving out of his way. The hopeful doe, again sniffing at the garden pickets, looked resentfully at Andy and bounced off. Four-Leaf, Clover and their brood of young were sporting in the watery slough. The setting sun cast long shadows of the dead trees across the swamp and the chickens were clucking sleepily. A balmy breeze ruffled the swamp grass. It was another summer night, exactly like summer nights had been for ages past and would be for ages to come.

Andy sighed and went into his house. He was discouraged and tired. For once, the swamp struck no responsive chord and the fact that he had come home failed to move him. He knelt to peer beneath the stove.

The fish had been eaten, but Frosty was still far under there and his warning growl rumbled. Andy got wearily to his feet. Obviously the kitten was not seriously injured and just as obviously any sort of enclosure, even a whole house, was far too much of a prison for his feline spirit. Too listless to have much appetite, Andy fixed himself a sandwich, washed it down with a glass of water, took the other fish heads from his icebox and put them on the porch.

Before he went to bed, he opened the door and propped it with a chunk of fire wood. He was attracted to Frosty and would like to keep him. But there would be no prisoners here; the kitten could have his freedom, if that was what he wanted.

Andy lay awake while the night wasted. Then sheer exhaustion made itself felt. He fell into deep slumber and did not rouse again until the sun was an hour high.

He sat up in bed to see Frosty settled in the still open doorway, washing his face with his front paws. Andy's dejection of yesterday melted away. He smiled.

"Well! So you decided to stay, after all!"

Frosty glanced at him and continued to wash his face.

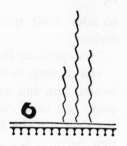

FROSTY PROWLS

Having his freedom, Frosty accepted it. Partly because the boy had set him free, he also accepted Andy. But there was another and very compelling reason why he had chosen to come back into the house, rather than escape into the swamp or the surrounding wilderness.

Perfectly capable of making his own way, entirely self-sufficient, he recognized no superior and would bow to no inferior. But he liked Andy and, in spite of the fact that he could do very well all by himself, he would not choose a lonely life, providing he could ally himself with an equal. If this fellow had kept him prisoner for a little while, he had also set him free and he had offered no real hurt. Frosty had recognized in Andy the same needs and urgencies that were so powerful within himself. They were traveling similar paths and it was well that they go together.

But it must be on a basis of strict equality, and because he was currently busy washing his face, Frosty continued to do so after Andy spoke to him. The young man's smile remained.

"Independent little devil, aren't you?"

His cleanup finished, Frosty sat down with his tail curled behind him and stared at the youth with unreadable feline eyes. Not until Andy swung out of bed and started across the floor did the kitten move. Then he went to meet his new partner, and arched his back and purred when Andy stooped to pet him. Thus, with a caress and a purr, their bargain was signed and sealed and both understood its terms.

While Andy prepared his breakfast, Frosty walked back out the open door and composed himself in the warming sun. He was not hungry, the fish heads and offal had been more than an adequate meal. While seeming to sleep, he inspected this new domain over which he had just become co-ruler.

Sporting in the slough, Four-Leaf and Clover and their family attracted his slight interest. They did not seem to be dangerous. They were creatures of the water, and, aside from its convenience when he was thirsty, Frosty had a violent aversion to water in all its forms. If he were hungry and happened to find a young muskrat on land, he might very well catch and kill one. Under no circumstances would he molest creatures in their sloughs and ponds.

While his eyes remained on the muskrat family, his ears were attuned to every sound. The various birdcalls he knew and because he did, he dismissed them as of little consequence. But when he heard the doe, that had gone to rest in some tall swamp grass, reach back to scratch an itching flank with a moist muzzle, he became instantly alert. He did not know the sound and he must know it.

Rising, Frosty slipped from the porch into the yard. He

had marked the doe, but though she remained the primary center of interest, he did not concentrate on her to the exclusion of all else. His first days in the hills had taught him that he could afford to neglect nothing on the ground and his recent grim experience with the owl was proof enough that he must also and at all times be aware of everything in the air. Because he was alert, Frosty saw the rattlesnake Andy had encountered last night before it saw him.

Still sluggish, digestion not yet complete, the snake had crawled to the lee of a boulder for the greater protection it offered against the night's chill. It coiled there, fearing little and scarcely interested in anything that happened.

Frosty soft-pawed a bit nearer. The snake was interesting and he had never before seen its like. Now was a good time to gauge its potentialities and discover for himself what manner of creature it might be. Guided by innate caution, the kitten halted three feet away and stared fixedly. Becoming alert, the snake rattled a warning.

Frosty listened, and having heard the sound, it was his. Watching the kitten with beady eyes, the snake ceased rattling. Frosty arched his back. He still did not know what manner of creature this might be, but whatever it was, he did not like it. Intending to discover for himself exactly what the snake could do, he remained cautious.

His feint, when he made it, was swift as only a cat's can be. His leap carried him to within fifteen inches of the forty-five inch snake and he nearly met disaster. The striking fangs came within a breath of brushing his fur! Having found out everything he wanted to know, Frosty withdrew.

The snake would strike and its swiftness equaled his own, but the kitten's anger increased. He had been challenged in his own territory. He would accept that challenge, but not blindly. A born warrior, he was also a born strategist.

The snake, rattling continuously now, undulated its thick body into coils. But though its strike was lightning fast, otherwise it was a comparatively sluggish thing. Frosty feinted again.

He knew to the exact hundredth of an inch the length of his last feint and this one he deliberately shortened. The snake struck, its venom-filled fangs falling just short, and Frosty became master of the situation. Knowing precisely how far the snake could strike, he feinted in rapid succession and each time teased the snake into hitting at him.

Finally, recognizing an *impasse* and rattling a warning as it did so, the snake started crawling away. Frosty leaped. He landed exactly where he had intended to land, just behind the head, where the snake's thick body tapered to a thin neck, and he bit even as he landed. His teeth met and almost in the same motion he leaped away.

For an interested moment he watched the quivering snake, now stretched full length. There were no death throes and no writhing coils, for Frosty had done exactly as he had planned to do and severed the spine. The reptile had died instantly. Forgetting the snake, Frosty padded on toward the doe.

Nearing her, he went into a stalk so stealthy and so silent that he crouched in the grass less than three feet away before she was aware of his presence. Her ears flicked forward and she opened alarmed eyes. Recognizing no threat, she relaxed and again scratched her flank with her muzzle. Satisfied because he had traced the source of this sound, the kitten retraced, almost step for step, the path he had taken coming into the grass and he was at the edge of the clearing when Andy emerged from the house.

Frosty did not show himself. Despite his liking for his human companion, he would not rush to meet him, as a dog might have, unless he felt like it, and right now he did not feel that way. Setting out to explore this new land, he wanted to do it in his own time and way and, for the present, he cared for no company.

Waiting until Andy was out of sight, he skirted the swamp and stopped to look closely at the muskrats, which were still swimming about in the slough. The parent animals moved farther out and eleven of their young followed. The twelfth, whose bump of curiosity was bigger than his portion of good sense, raised in the water for a better look at this fascinating creature, then swam eagerly toward him. Head extended, nostrils quivering, eyes bright, he climbed out on the bank.

The kitten stared back haughtily. Bigger than the baby muskrat, he still was not hungry enough to hunt. Besides, obviously the muskrats were lesser creatures. Frosty considered them as belonging in almost the same category as the rabbits that almost always ran. He went around the slough and into the swamp.

The tall grass waved over his head, so that he could see only that which lay directly about him. Nor could he smell very much because the over-all dank odor of the swamp drowned slighter scents. A mink or fox would have detected them and sought out their sources, if they were interested enough to do so. A cat could not, but Frosty's matchless ears took the place of both eyes and nose. He heard the flutter of a bird's wing, marked it down and deliberated. Having fed, he'd still accept a choice tidbit should one come his way. He stalked the bird and found it in a patch of grass.

It was a sora. Coming here to feed on seeds, it had entangled one foot in a slim strip of wire-tough swamp grass and, in struggling to free itself, had succeeded only in tangling the other foot. Almost exhausted, it was able to do little save flutter its wings.

Frosty pounced upon the bird, killed it and ate as much as he wanted. His belly filled, he sought a warm place and curled up to rest. But he was careful to choose a napping place roofed with interlaced tops of swamp grass. There were enemies in the air, but it stood to reason that they could not catch him if they were unable to see him.

In spite of the fact that he was hidden, at no time did he sleep so soundly that he was oblivious to what went on and again his ears served him. Something that splashed in a nearby slough had to be a leaping fish; swimming muskrats seldom splashed or did anything else to attract attention to themselves. From far off came a loud noise; one of the dead swamp trees had finally toppled.

Frosty alerted himself only when he heard a sound he did not know. It was not loud but neither was it especially muted, as though some small creature that did not care whether or not it was seen moved through the swamp. At length it arose near the remains of the sora. Silent as a shadow, Frosty stalked forward. Even before he reached what was left of the bird, he heard something eating.

He looked through an aperture in the grass to see a creature approximately the size of a large cat, contentedly feasting on the remains of the sora. It was lustrous-black, except for a V-shaped patch of white on its head that became two white stripes which ran to the base of its tail. This silky tail was heavily furred, the feet were short and stubby. Frosty stared with vast curiosity.

Suddenly, and almost without visible motion, he flattened

himself where he was and held perfectly still. A day-cruising
great horned owl, which Frosty had seen at all only because
he was wholly alert, floated in to seize the feeding animal.
The owl winged low over the swamp with his prey.

Frosty sneezed and raced violently away, for suddenly
the air was nauseous with stink so thick that a knife might
almost have cut it. Obviously the owl didn't mind at all,
but to Frosty it was a repulsive odor. However, he had
learned something else; no matter where they were encountered or what they were doing, skunks were better left
alone. After running a hundred yards, Frosty continued at
a fast walk. The air still reeked and he wanted to get away
from the stench. As soon as he had gone far enough so that
there was only faint evidence of the unfortunate skunk's
fate, he resumed prowling.

The swamp interested him greatly and he wanted to learn
as much as possible about it. Because exploration was currently more fascinating than fighting, he detoured around
another rattlesnake and continued on his way. He mounted
a little rise that was literally honeycombed with the burrows
of striped gophers and stopped to watch.

Flitting from their burrows, the gophers were feasting
upon a veritable inundation of grasshoppers that had come
among them. Moving like an animated streak, one of them
would pounce upon a grasshopper and at once dodge back
to its burrow or into the shelter of some huckleberry brush
that grew upon the knoll. The wise little animals never
exposed themselves for more than a few seconds at a time,
for they knew too well the many perils that threatened.

As Frosty watched the gophers, disaster struck them.

Another rattlesnake, lying like a strip of carelessly discarded velvet upon the little rise, struck a gopher when it paused nearby to snatch up a grasshopper. Forgetting his grasshopper, the stricken animal bounced toward his burrow. But he no longer moved like a streak. The injected venom made itself felt almost at once, and instead of ducking into his refuge, the gopher crawled down it.

After a moment, in no hurry at all and following his quarry by the scent it left on the ground, the snake moved sluggishly on the gopher's trail, finally disappearing down the burrow which the stricken creature had entered.

Frosty circled the little rise and went on. He was far too well-fed even to think of hunting the gophers, but the colony was something to remember when he should be hungry. Any rodent at all was not only acceptable but desirable food.

Coming to a slough, Frosty slunk like a wraith along its edge and sank down to watch a baby muskrat. Visible only from the bank upon which the kitten crouched, hidden from every other direction by a curl of overhanging grass, the youngster was busily engaged in digging succulent bulbs from the mud on the bank's far side. Thus Frosty learned what even Andy had not yet discovered.

This baby belonged to the cautious pair that knew so well how to protect themselves, and evidently he had inherited his parents' caution. Already anticipating another litter, the parents were separating themselves from the first one. The muskrats were doing exactly as Andy had hoped they'd do and spreading out.

Little interested, Frosty resumed his travels and found himself on a point of land that jutted into the slough. He paused, looking at the six feet of water that lay before him. He could not jump it and he would never swim unless forced to do so, therefore he did the only thing he could do and retraced his steps. Continuing around the slough, he came to a blanket of tangled weeds that covered it and crossed on them. Anything heavier, or even heavier-footed, would have fallen through. Frosty not only proceeded in perfect safety but knew he was safe.

He came to a little stream, one of the few clear-running streams in the swamp, and watched a mother mallard and her brood of seven swim happily there. Frosty did not molest them. No wanton killer, he would hunt only when he wanted to eat. But the mallard family was something else to remember should he be hungry and in their vicinity.

When night fell, he was still in the swamp and entirely unconcerned about it. This was, perhaps, even a little more to his liking for he was a little more a creature of night than day.

Frosty halted suddenly. He was in an area which, being heavily browsed by swamp deer, had comparatively short grass. Deer moved about, chewing noisily and now and then blowing to clear their nostrils of a bit of dust. But there was something more and the kitten strained to discover its identity.

He saw the deer more clearly than a human being would have but not as clearly as he himself would have seen them by day. Though his night vision was good, he had no magic lens that pierced the darkness and made everything easily visible. Besides the deer and the chewed-down grass, he could see nothing. He could hear only the deer moving, chewing, blowing, and the soft murmur of the wind that never seemed to cease. He still knew that danger threatened.

The knowledge came to him, probably. through a very

faint sound that tickled his built-in ear antennae, without identifying itself and without even seeming like an audible noise. Had he had any clear idea of what he faced now, he would have known what to do about it. Lacking any idea whatsoever, he could only be careful.

He turned away from the sound and went back into tall grass. Once there, where he was at least partially shielded from great horned owls, he broke into a fast run. But it was not a panicky run. He had set out to elude something which he realized existed, and that was all he knew about it. No instinct could possibly help him and blind flight could lead to nothing but trouble. In a situation such as this, his only hope lay in relying on planned intelligence.

Frosty halted after running three hundred yards and turned to face the direction from which he had come. He had scurried into a part of the swamp which he had not yet visited. This was an error, and almost instantly he knew it was an error. Every tree, clump of brush and the various kinds of grass through which he had already prowled were clearly mapped in his brain. He should have gone back there because, in the event of an emergency, he would have known exactly what lay around him and precisely how he might take advantage of the terrain. But it was too late to turn now.

He could hear nothing save the wind, a group of barred owls talking to each other in some of the dead trees, and suddenly, far off, the death shriek of a rabbit upon which a mink had pounced. He still knew there was danger, and that it was on his trail. He ran on.

Suddenly he came to a slough, a thirty-foot-wide stretch of water whose surface eerily reflected the dim light that filtered from stars. Six feet out, a group of dead trees reared skeleton trunks and rattled their bare bones of branches. Frosty turned again.

He was not trapped, for he could run in either direction along the slough's bank, but that would be blind running and he did not know where it might lead him. Now was the time for planning, and before he did anything else, he wanted to know from exactly what he fled. Suddenly he did know.

It was another coyote, for presently he heard it, and it was on his trail. He could not know that it was a young beast which, catching the scent of a cat and eager to renew the age-old cat and dog fight, had flung itself pell-mell along that scent. Frosty made ready to fight.

He saw the coyote emerge from the grass and run headlong at him. Crouching, prepared to spring, his nerve broke suddenly. Turning, he leaped blindly for the trunk of the nearest tree, missed by eighteen inches, fell into the slough and went under.

Surfacing, he knew only seething fury. Water was the most distasteful of all places to him. Being forced ignominiously to fall into it roused all his warrior blood, but even now he did not attack blindly.

Striking for the bank, he saw the eager coyote waiting for him and marked its position exactly. When his paws found a footing, he sprang at once and his body arched into the air. Again he went to the head, scraping with all four paws, even while he sliced with his teeth. The startled coyote—a veteran would have known exactly what to do—stood for one brief second. Then it gave a startled yelp, unseated its attacker with a fling of its head and streaked away.

Frosty waited long enough to assure himself that his enemy was not coming back. Once he was positive of that, he meticulously groomed his wet fur and started toward the house.

I now waited long enough to assure himself that his enemy was not coming back. Once he was positive of that, he meticulously groomed his wet fur and started toward the house.

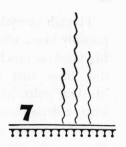

7

THE SECOND PLANTING

Visiting the game warden, Joe Wilson, and listening to his old friend's sage advice had started Andy on a whole fresh train of thought and furnished new ideas. He sat at the table in his little house and devoted himself to serious thinking.

Muskrat pelts were fairly valuable in the fall, as soon as the weather turned cold enough to make them so. But they were far and away at their best, and brought the highest prices, if taken in late winter or early spring. In order to realize the maximum profit from his venture—and even to think about anything else would be silly—the entire crop of pelts would have to be harvested in a comparatively short time. This posed a problem which, until now, Andy had not even considered.

Nor had he thought of sharing with his neighbors, he admitted honestly. He now saw this as a near necessity, aside from being a kindly gesture.

Though everything looked favorable, as yet he could not possibly know whether his plan to turn the swamp into one big muskrat ranch would end in success or failure. But he did know that there could be no intermediate point. Muskrat pelts, which, depending on the fur market, might bring a little more or a little less than two dollars each—and probably would average that—were not so valuable that a few, or even a few dozen, would be worthwhile. He had to take a great many. But if he restricted himself to the best part of the trapping season—even though he worked as many hours as possible seven days a week during that time—how many pelts would one man, working alone, be able to handle? Without knowing the limit, he was sure that there had to be one.

Merely setting enough traps and moving them whenever a sufficient number of muskrats had been taken from any one portion of the swamp would, within itself, be no small task. In fact, though most of it could be done before trapping started, just patrolling the swamp and deciding how many pelts might safely be taken, and still leave an adequate foundation breeding stock, would be a big job. Then there would be skinning the catch, making stretching boards and stretching the pelts. All of this not only had to be done, but it must be well done. A poorly cleansed or badly stretched pelt was not worth nearly as much as one cared for expertly.

It would be to his benefit—and theirs, too—if he accepted Joe Wilson's advice and asked the Casman brothers and Old Man Haroldson and his sons whether they cared to participate. Since Andy was furnishing the swamp, all the initial investment and all the basic work, it would be feasible and acceptable to work something out on a share basis. It would, naturally, be useless to ask Luke Trull to cooperate with anybody in anything. Andy caught up a stub of pencil and a scratch pad and began to figure.

He had planted twelve muskrats, of which he had six, two pairs and two lone females, left. They had produced thirty-eight young, and though Andy could not be sure—he had found the remains of two baby muskrats without identifying what had killed them—he thought that at least thirty remained. He intended to plant twenty more mated pairs, and judging from past experience, he could expect to lose half of them. If the rest, and supposing ten females survived, propagated in proportion to the first planting, there would be somewhat more than ninety young. If each adult female produced at least one more litter—

Andy threw his pencil down and stared across the table. So many factors entered into the picture that there was about as much possibility of accurately forecasting how much increase there would be as there was of knowing definitely which cow in a herd would switch its tail to the left first. If he could keep furred and feathered predators down and Luke Trull out, and if he were lucky, there might be any- where between 150 and 200 muskrats in the swamp with the coming of spring. That would not be nearly enough to start reaping a harvest of pelts. It wouldn't even be an adequate breeding stock, and perhaps there would not be enough muskrats to start trapping the following spring. But by the third year, always assuming that luck was on his side, the venture should show at least a modest return.

At any rate, he would see Ira and Jud Casman and Old Man Haroldson and his five strapping sons in the near future. He would explain what he was doing and what he hoped to do and he would point out that, if he had their co-operation, which he thought he'd get, nobody would become rich but there would be something for all who cared to join in. Coming in the spring, when other work was slack, such funds would be welcome. Luke Trull was and would have to remain Andy's problem.

Rising, the boy walked to the window and peered into the darkness. He hadn't seen the frost-coated kitten since early morning, and in addition to anxiety, he felt an unaccountable sense of disappointment. Somewhat irritably, he tried to shrug it away. Why should he have sensed a powerful bond between the kitten and himself? And why was he forever getting ideas and fancies which no one else seemed ever to entertain? Obviously the kitten, at best a half-wild thing, had gone back into the wilderness out of which it had come. That was its privilege.

Andy resumed his seat at the table and again took up his pencil and scratch pad. A second time he started calculating as to exactly what was going to happen, and a second time he gave it up as useless. He'd thought everything was carefully planned and well executed, but all the books he had read and all the information at his disposal, while definitely valuable, could at the very best only help guide him. No book ever written could tell him exactly what muskrats would do in his swamp, for the simple reason that there had never before been any muskrats there. Though he would certainly apply what he already knew, experience alone could teach him the rest. Andy started suddenly.

He listened, sure he'd heard the cry of a cat, but when the sound was not repeated he decided he had heard only the wind whining around a corner of his house. Two minutes later, and there was no mistake this time, he heard the cry again. He walked to the door, opened it, and Frosty padded in.

As meticulously clean as though he had done nothing all day long except groom himself, tail erect and eyes friendly, but at the same time managing to preserve his own great dignity, he came straight to Andy and arched against his legs. But when Andy stooped to pick him up, the frost-coated kitten dodged aside. He retreated about four feet, sat down on the floor with his tail curled around his legs and regarded Andy with grave eyes.

Understanding, Andy grinned. Some cats might love to be fondled and cuddled, but obviously Frosty was not one of them. He was a partner, not a possession, and his were a partner's rights. The boy's grin widened. Again, as he had this morning, he saw something about this proud kitten that fitted exactly his own ideas. Independent, intelligent and spirited, Frosty knew what he wanted and what he did not want, and certainly he wanted no condescension or patronizing. Andy spoke to him.

"I don't know where you've been all day, Frosty, but wherever it was, you should be hungry now. How about some grub?"

He himself had dined on chicken, and he took a leg from the cold remains that were stored in his icebox. Cutting the meat away from the bone, he laid it on a clean saucer and placed the saucer on the floor. After a moment's grave deliberation, Frosty padded forward and ate daintily. He cleaned his face and whiskers and came over to settle himself near Andy's chair. The closed door and the fact that he was shut in were of little importance, for he had satisfied himself that the door would be opened again.

Purring, he gave himself over to slumber as sound as he would ever enjoy after Andy had reached down to stroke him gently. He would never be satisfied always to stay in the house; he had large ideas which called for ample space in which to execute them. But again he had found a refuge. As long as he was in the house, he need not be constantly alert, for no danger threatened here.

Andy picked up a magazine devoted to furs and fur raising and thumbed through it, but his mind was not on the printed pages. When encroaching civilization forced them to change their way of life, the Gates clan had scattered. But two of the Gates clan, Andy and his father, had been unable to leave the swamp. It was a home to which they were bound by unbreakable ties—but it was also a way of life that nobody else would have chosen and nobody at all understood. Even to the hillmen, far closer to it than any town dweller could possibly be, anyone who elected deliberately to live in the swamp was throwing his life away.

Andy could not live elsewhere, but he knew suddenly that his life had taken a turn for the better. He not only had a companion, but one that had chosen of its own free will to join him. In addition, although Andy had no way of knowing where Frosty had been, it went without saying that he must have been prowling somewhere, and his new partner was evidently not only able to cope with but to triumph over the rigors and challenges that such a life offered. Andy needed to know no more.

After a while he rose, undressed, gave himself a sponge bath with warm water from the stove's reservoir, put on his pajamas and went to bed. He lay wakeful in the darkness, and when something jumped on the bed he put out a hand to touch Frosty. He smiled contentedly and went to sleep.

Andy was up with the dawn, and as he built a fire in the kitchen stove he started pondering a new problem that faced him. His own way of life had for so long been so well worked out that it had fallen into a routine pattern. In summer, since he had only an icebox and visited the town infrequently, he never bought fresh meat which he himself would be unable to use before it spoiled. He depended on staples, ham and bacon, a very few canned meats, eggs, fish from the swamp, an occasional chicken and vegetables from his garden. After hunting season opened and icy weather set in, he froze the game he shot and occasionally he purchased from or traded with the Casman brothers or one of the Haroldsons for a side of pork. Having Frosty meant that he must make provision for him, but it was not an urgent matter and it could be taken care of when he went into town. Possibly he would buy some cans of commercial cat food to supplement what he already had to offer.

Andy breakfasted on eggs, opened a can of milk for Frosty and washed the dishes. Frosty slipped out with him and composed himself on the porch when his companion left the house. Andy gave him a farewell pat and set his face toward the Casman brothers' farm.

Ira and Jud, bachelors, lived two miles back in the hills. The various abandoned farms Andy passed on his way to them were sufficient evidence that, in their own way, the Casman brothers were as hard as the granite boulders that reared humped gray backs out of their fields and pastures.

The Gateses had not been the only ones to leave the hills. Many of the Casmans and Haroldsons, and all the Trulls excepting Luke, had gone, too. Ira and Jud, like Old Man Haroldson and his sons, had not only managed to hang on but even did quite well. They never had more than modest sums of money, but they never knew want either, and they were happy with the life they led.

Andy passed the one-room, one-teacher country school which he had attended and which was now kept open solely for the numerous offspring of Old Man Haroldson's sons. He swung up a hill, descended the other side and saw the Casman farm.

The house and outbuildings were well back from the dirt road. Five cattle and about sixty sheep grazed in a pasture and the fields were green with various crops. Andy swung up the lane toward the house and the Casmans' big, friendly dog—there were far fewer rattlesnakes away from the swamp —bounded forward. He barked a happy welcome and Andy stooped to pet him. Straightening, he saw Jud Casman standing in the doorway.

Jud was lean as a greyhound, tough as an oak knot, suspicious and approximately as talkative as a wary buck. There was no certain way to determine his age. He had taken an active part in the Trull-Casman-Gates feud, but, like Andy, he knew that belonged to the past. He murmured,

"Mawnin', Andy."

"Good morning, Jud."

"You et?"

"I've had breakfast, Jud. I've come to talk with you and to ask something from you and Ira."

"Ira's afield. Call him in if'n you like."

"That isn't necessary. You can tell him. I'm trying to do something in my swamp. Now—"

Andy described his project. He spoke of the muskrats he had already liberated, and of the increase in them. He told of the twenty pairs that were due in a few days. If the plan worked, Andy said, it would work very well—so well, in fact, that he would need help. Therefore, he would share with any hillman who cared to join him. He himself must retain complete control and he would say how many muskrats might be taken from any one section of the swamp. It would be the trapper's job to take the muskrats, pelt them and stretch the pelts. For so doing, he would receive half the value of such pelts as he handled and Andy would do the marketing.

Jud listened in attentive silence. When Andy was finished, he spoke. "What you want of Ira'n me?"

"A chance," Andy said frankly, "and nothing more. The best way I can figure it, there won't even be an adequate breeding stock next spring. There can't possibly be any trapping; maybe there can't even be any the following spring. But we should be able to start the spring following that. All I want from you, or anyone, is to leave the muskrats alone until the time is right."

"Me'n Ira got no call to pester 'em."

"Thanks, Jud."

"*M-mm.* You're gittin' twenty mo' these mushrats?"

"Forty. Twenty mated pairs."

"Quite a passel to tote."

"I'll make three trips."

"You needn't," Jud declared. "Come get our Tom horse.

He packs good an' just turn him loose when you're done. He'll come home."

Andy led Tom, the Casman brothers' gentle brown pack horse, off the road and down the trail to his house. The halter rope was slack. Tom knew he had a job and was entirely willing to do it. Sure-footed as a goat, he threaded his way among the boulders in his path and matched his pace to Andy's. Since it was unnecessary to watch the horse, Andy gave himself to reflection.

There was a change in his relations with the Casman brothers and Old Man Haroldson and his sons. Nobody had mentioned it and it could not be seen, but it could be felt. His reception by each of the Haroldsons had been approximately the same as that which the Casmans had accorded him. None had been loquacious, but all had listened and all had promised to leave Andy's muskrats alone until he himself gave the word. Through that simple understanding, the change was worked.

Formerly considered at least queer, if not an outright crackpot, he had now advanced to being respected. Nobody except himself had thought his swamp anything except a worthless marsh. He had not only seen possibilities there but was in the process of developing them. Time might very well prove that it was they, not he, who had been short-sighted.

When he arrived at his house, Andy tied Tom to the porch railing. Frosty, napping in the sun, glided silkily over, regarded the horse with haughty and the muskrats with haughtier disdain, then sat down to watch the proceedings Unstrapping the ropes that bound the crates to Tom's pack saddle, Andy lifted them to the ground, one by one. When they were all unloaded, he untied Tom, looped the lead rope through his bridle so it wouldn't drag and patted him on the rump. The horse started cheerfully up the trail toward his home.

These muskrats were designed for the most inaccessible ponds and sloughs in the swamp and it was too late even to think of taking them in today. Two at a time, one under each arm, Andy carried the crates inside. He stepped back to look at them with pleased satisfaction.

An almost visible sneer on his face, Frosty paraded up and down the row of crates, looked intently at the occupants of each and turned loftily away. Andy laughed.

"I take it you don't think they're your social equals?"

Disdaining to glance again at the crated muskrats, Frosty curled up in his favorite place near Andy's chair. He lost himself in his own meditations and the young man gave him an affectionate glance. The further this partnership progressed, the better he liked it.

Andy was up and had breakfasted before daylight. He let Frosty out and then gave his attention to the muskrats. Twenty crates meant four loads of five crates each. That many was by no means a heavy pack, but it was as much as could be carried comfortably through the swamp. Besides, Andy had in mind four different sections of the swamp where he wanted to plant these animals. Strapping five crates to his pack board, he went outside.

Always before, as soon as he was let out of the house, Frosty had gone about his own affairs of the day and usually Andy had not seen him again until after nightfall. This morning he was surprised to find the kitten still waiting, and even more astonished when Frosty fell in beside him. Andy raised puzzled brows.

"What are you aiming to do here, fella?"

Tail high, eyes friendly, Frosty stayed beside him. Andy grinned good-naturedly. Dogs were supposed to accompany their masters wherever they went, but nobody expected a cat to do so. However, this one had evidently made up his mind to go along and he was welcome. Maybe, Andy thought whimsically, he wants to see for himself what is going to happen to the muskrats.

Andy made his way toward the north end of the swamp, a wild and tangled place, with not too many sloughs and ponds but more trees and brush than any other part of the whole area. It was also the most dangerous part of the swamp because safe trails were few. The boy worked his way through a tangle of brush and came to a slough.

He stopped. Frosty halted beside him and Andy looked speculatively at his companion. So far, the kitten had shown not the slightest desire to let himself be handled or to permit any undue familiarity. But when Andy stooped and picked him up, Frosty settled contentedly in his arms. Safe on the other side of the slough, of his own accord he jumped down.

Andy grinned in appreciation. While respecting his own self, Frosty had no objection to hitchhiking when that was in order. He'd known very well that Andy could carry him securely across the slough. Again on the ground, he paced contentedly beside his partner.

He sat on the bank and watched solemnly when Andy released the first pair of muskrats in a weed-grown pond. Confused at first, the liberated animals quickly gave way to the usual wild delight and for the next few moments devoted themselves to sporting in the slough. Then, swimming to the bank, they began to satisfy their hunger. Aside from keeping a wary eye on Andy, they made no attempt to hide and offered not the slightest indication that they knew danger might lurk here.

Andy went on. Previous experience had taught him that, with rare exceptions, pen-raised muskrats—and probably most other pen-raised creatures—would react in just this fashion. Never having known danger, they could not possibly understand that it existed. But they would learn if they escaped the first few perils that threatened, and though some would surely die, some would live.

Making his way to the next slough, where once more Frosty watched gravely, Andy released another pair of muskrats. He liberated a third pair, and was about to free a fourth when he discovered that the kitten was no longer beside him. Andy swung to look for his companion.

Thirty yards away, Frosty had leaped to the top of a moss-covered boulder and flattened himself on it. His tail was straight behind him, and he was so still that not even a hair rippled. His attitude was one of watchful alertness.

The short hairs on the back of Andy's neck rippled and he had a presentiment of danger. At once he dismissed it. There were plenty of dangers in the swamp, but he knew all of them and understood how to cope with them. Still, Frosty had heard or sensed something of which he remained unaware. Andy started toward him. He had covered less than half the distance when the kitten slipped from the boulder, melted into the brush, and disappeared.

A second time, Andy had a premonition of danger and a second time he forced it from his mind. Certainly, Frosty knew something he did not know. However, it was not only possible but highly probable that the kitten might be greatly alarmed by something which would not trouble him at all. Andy strained to hear a rattlesnake or to see evidence of a coyote, bobcat, great horned owl, or anything else that might have frightened Frosty.

He could neither see nor hear anything at all, and anxiety for the kitten rose within him. He was not greatly concerned about whatever had caused his partner to flee. Frosty had lived in the wilderness a long while and the very fact that he had lived was evidence that he knew how to stay alive. But as far as Andy knew, the only ways out of this section of the swamp led across sloughs and he was certain that, of his own accord, Frosty would not cross water. Therefore, unless he could be found, he was marooned here.

Andy hurried to liberate his two remaining pairs of muskrats, then hastened back to the boulder upon which Frosty had crouched. He called,

"Frosty."

There was no response and the boy's anxiety mounted. He'd lived with his partner long enough to assure himself that the quality which he had first seen in Frosty was indeed a part of him. The kitten was not only capable of deciding for himself and acting as he felt best, but once he had made up his mind to do a certain thing, he would do it and nothing whatever would swerve him. Even though he heard his friend calling, he would respond only if he was satisfied that that was the proper thing to do. Andy began methodically to cast back and forth.

An hour and a half later, he gave up the search as hopeless. No human could find a cat that did not want to be found, and the day was wasting. The boy hurried hopefully back to the slough over which he had carried Frosty. But the frost-coated kitten was not waiting for him. Andy deliberated.

He should turn back and resume the hunt for his partner.

Sooner or later, no matter where he hid or what his reason for hiding was, when that reason no longer existed, Frosty would show himself. At the same time, and aside from their practical value, he had an obligation to the remaining musk-rats. They'd been imprisoned in the little crates for as long as anything should be, and it was only right and just to release them. Andy made up his mind.

Hurrying back to the house, he strapped five more crates on the pack board and took them into the swamp. He did not stop for lunch because he wanted to finish as soon as possible and go look for Frosty. He took a third load and went back for the last one.

These he carried to a remote but relatively open section of the swamp. There were few trees and little brush here, but swamp grass grew tall and the ponds and sloughs were choked with succulent aquatic growth that would enable his released captives to live richly. He freed four pairs and was about to liberate a fifth when he straightened.

Again, and for no apparent reason, he felt a strong sense of danger. The short hairs on his neck resumed prickling. Something was indeed in the swamp, but it was not stalking Frosty. It was on his trail.

Andy whirled suddenly to see Luke Trull, who had been peering cautiously over the swamp grass, throw himself down in it.

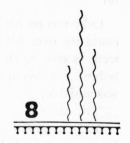

8

MAROONED

Acting as though he had seen nothing, Andy put his remaining cage of muskrats beside the slough that was to be their future home. He knelt, opened the cage, spilled the muskrats into the slough and watched them swim bewilderedly about. Casually, for Luke Trull was crafty as any fox that had ever padded through the swamp, he strapped the empty crate on his pack board and slipped into the shoulder straps.

He turned as if intending to retrace exactly the path he had followed. The swamp grass was tall and dense. A man who wanted to crawl away would do so if his suspicions were aroused and have every chance of hiding successfully. When the path had brought him as near as possible to the place where he had seen Luke Trull duck into the grass, Andy shucked the pack board from his shoulder and ran as swiftly as possible toward the spot. A moment later, he looked down on the hillman.

103

Luke was on his hands and knees. His head turned so he could see over his shoulder, and the eyes that met Andy's were as cold as those of any hunting great horned owl or bobcat. But his lips framed an appeasing smile and his voice was amiable,

"Hi, Andy."

Andy stood still, for the moment unable to speak. Fierce, hot anger mingled with almost complete discouragement. Even though he had taken the Casmans and the Haroldsons into his confidence, it had still been a grave mistake to bring the muskrats in by day, for Luke Trull had seen and Luke had known. The boy licked dry lips.

When he had left the house this morning, it had never occurred to him that he might be followed and therefore he had been off guard. Of course he shouldn't have been, but it was too late to think of that now. Since he had failed to be alert, any hillman who cared to do so, while remaining unobserved himself, could have followed him wherever he went.

Andy knew now why Frosty had hidden. Luke must have been on his trail from the very first. He himself had not only shown the fellow the safe paths into the swamp, but Luke knew where everyone of these twenty pairs of muskrats were planted. It went without saying that he would know how to find them again, and probably he would be able to find the others. Andy bit off his words and spat them at the crouching man,

"I told you to stay out of my swamp!"

"Why now, you never told me nothin' like that."

"What are you doing here?"

"Lookin'."

"Get up, Luke!"

"Now, Andy, mought's well be neighborly. You give leave to Ira'n Jud Casman an' all the Haroldsons to help ya trap mushrats. All I come out for was to see why ya fo'got to ask me?"

It was a flimsy excuse. Luke knew well enough where Andy lived, and if he had wanted to ask him anything at all, he might easily have come to his house. Any farfetched chance that he might actually have followed Andy into the swamp to ask about anything at all was refuted by the fact that he had been hiding in the grass. Andy's voice was dangerously low-pitched,

"Get up, Luke!"

"Not afore ya cool a mite."

Andy reached down, grasped the other's coat collar, jerked him erect and spun him around. When he swung, the blow started at the tips of his toes and traveled through his clenched fist. He connected squarely, and Luke Trull sat down suddenly in the grass.

Supporting himself with both arms, he looked intently at Andy. His eyes remained cold and the smile was gone. Andy spoke quietly,

"Get out! Don't come back!"

Without a word, Luke Trull rose and shuffled away. Andy had a sudden cold feeling. Luke Trull was no more ethical than a rattlesnake, and he was far more dangerous. Andy knew that the man would come again, but he would not be caught again. Nor would he ever forget this. One way or another, he would have his revenge, and if he confined his vengeance to wiping out the muskrat colonies, Andy would be lucky.

The boy's courage returned. He had known when he

planned his muskrat ranch that it would be no easy task
and that he would have to fight for it, so fight he would.

Andy picked up his pack board and in what remained of
the day went back to the place where Frosty had disappeared.
He searched carefully but he could not find the kitten, and
when he returned to the house, Frosty was not there. The
boy dawdled over a skimpy supper and went dispiritedly to
bed.

Rising at daybreak, Andy hurried eagerly to the door and
called, but his frost-coated partner did not respond. Pondering the advisability of going again to look for him, he decided that it would be a waste of time. He'd already covered
that whole section very thoroughly without finding a trace
of the kitten. Frosty would be found when and if he was
ready.

Andy was on the point of going into the swamp to check on
the muskrats he had planted yesterday, but he caught up a
hoe instead and went to his garden. Sadly neglected for too
long, weeds were crowding vegetables. Andy hoed his way
down the aisles in his onion patch. Putting the hoe aside, he
knelt to pull the weeds that were growing among the onions.

Hearing a car on the road, he merely glanced up briefly,
then resumed his weeding. He expected no visitors, certainly
none who might drive a car.

Suddenly a crisp voice asked, "Is your name Gates?"

Andy turned, startled, and rose to confront a young man
who wore a State Policeman's uniform. Reserved and doing
his best to uphold both the dignity and the authority of his
position, nevertheless the young trooper could not completely
hide a sparkle in his eye and a humorous twist to his mouth.
Andy said,

"I'm Gates."

"Andrew Gates?"

"That's right."

"I have a warrant for your arrest."

Andy gave way to astonishment. "A what?"

"Do you want me to read it to you?"

"What's it about?"

"An assault warrant sworn out by a man named Trull. Let's see," the trooper glanced at the warrant, "Luke Trull."

Andy clenched his jaws. Joe Wilson, who had said that Luke would not fight back, but would go to the State Police if Andy hit him, had known exactly what he was talking about.

The trooper looked steadily at Andy. "Well?"

"That's right."

"You assaulted this Trull character?"

"Yes."

"And you admit it?"

"I admit it."

The trooper turned quizzical. "Why?"

"I found him in my swamp."

"Is the swamp posted?"

"No."

"Did he threaten you?"

"No."

"Yours was a wilful attack?"

"Yes."

"Have you nothing to say in your own defense?"

Andy answered wearily, "It would take too long. You'd have to know Luke Trull."

The trooper, who never should have done so and never would have done so had he been more experienced, grinned. "I'll have to take you in."

"Okeh. I'll just let my chickens out to forage."

Side by side, a somehow awkward silence between them, they walked to the chicken pen and then on to the trooper's parked car. The officer made a U-turn and started toward town. He asked suddenly,

"What do you want in that swamp?"

"Quite a few things."

"This Trull—seems to me I've seen his name on our records—what's he want there?"

"Something that belongs to me."

"Did he steal from you?"

"No."

"I don't get it."

"He's going to steal. I planted muskrats in the swamp. He followed me to find out where they are."

The trooper said thoughtfully, "Oh!"

For five minutes they drove in silence. The officer broke it with, "I can take you before Justice Benton, one of the best."

Andy said, "Okeh."

"One of the best," the trooper emphasized. "Have you ever been arrested before?"

"No!"

"Then you can't know court procedure," the policeman said. "Now Benton is a great jurist. He's really wasting himself in a small town. He spends most of his time studying the decisions of various high courts, including the Supreme Court, and deciding what he might have done were he to rule on the same point of law. He shouldn't be handling minor cases and he knows it, and it irritates him if one takes up his time. He always wants to lay it on with a heavy hand when that happens, and he could send you to jail. On the other hand, when a defendant's reasonable and admits his guilt, Benton's usually inclined to go light. Now you've already told me you're guilty and I'll have to testify as to that. Do you understand?"

Andy grinned his appreciation. The trooper, in the only way he possibly could, was telling him how to get off lightly. Andy said,

"I understand."

An hour later, he faced Judge Benton, a stern-faced little man who had a disconcerting habit of peering over instead of through his glasses. The trooper recited the charges. Justice Benton glanced briefly at the papers pertaining to the case and turned to Andy,

"How does the defendant plead?"

"Guilty," Andy murmured.

"Young man," Justice Benton said sternly, "in flouting the laws of this great state, you have set yourself above the whole people whose duly elected representatives formulate those laws. However, you are youthful and the court is not unaware of the fact that youth is too often prompted by passion and inexperience. So the maximum sentence shall not be imposed. At the same time, you receive fair warning that henceforth you are to keep the peace with this plaintiff whom you have so grievously wronged. Nor must your present breach of the law go unpunished. In lieu of fine, this court sentences you to—"

Justice Benton paused dramatically, then finished,

"Ten days in jail."

Whimsically deciding that Frosty wanted to accompany him into the swamp so he could see for himself what happened to the muskrats, Andy would never be aware of the fact that a chance shot had hit the mark. The kitten was curious about the muskrats' fate, but above and beyond that, he wanted something else. In electing to become Andy's partner, he had chosen much better than he knew. Self-sufficient and willing to surrender none of his independence, the partnership had been affected by a circumstance over which he had not the slightest control. Liking Andy and wanting a strong ally of his caliber, Frosty had come to love his partner.

A confirmed prowler, he would continue to prowl and to go his own way whenever that seemed expedient. But he went gladly back to the house and eagerly looked forward to meeting Andy when he arrived. There were even times when he voluntarily cut his prowling short to have his partner's company. He also went into the swamp partly because Andy was going there.

He became aware that they were being followed shortly after Andy planted the third pair of muskrats, but at first all he knew was that something trailed him. Uneasy backward glances and growing nervousness were lost on his friend, who was intent on getting his work done. This was wholly understandable, for it never occurred to Frosty that Andy was responsible for him, any more than he was obligated to watch out for his partner. Never for an instant questioning that he was well able to take care of himself, he never doubted that his partner could do likewise. Finally, able to bear the tension no longer, Frosty had to find out for himself just who was trailing them.

His ears had already informed him that it was a man. No fox, bobcat, coyote, or anything else that belonged to the wild, had ever walked so heavily or so clumsily. Blowing against him, the wind brought no identifying scent to his nose. Frosty sprang to the boulder's top because it was a vantage point from which, while he still used his ears, he could use his eyes to better advantage.

He had one fleeting glimpse of their pursuer just after Andy turned. Two hundred yards behind them, to the side instead of directly on their tail, Luke Trull saw Andy turn and dropped behind a boulder. Frosty unsheathed and sheathed his claws while his tail twitched angrily.

He knew this man as an enemy much more deadly than any other he had ever faced. Even the great horned owl that had seized him had worked less injury than Luke Trull. Vividly Frosty remembered the ride, tortured hours in the sack before the coyote came to release him, and the hardships after that. But there was something more. The various creatures that would have killed and eaten Frosty had merely been pursuing life in the only way they could live it. Luke Trull had belittled him and struck at his pride. But he was powerful, and though Frosty did not fear him, it was prudent to avoid a battle. He slipped from the boulder, drifted into thick brush and waited.

When Andy came back and called, Frosty remained in hiding. This was his affair and he expected no other living thing ever to fight in his behalf, but neither could he be guided by any judgment save his own. At the same time, he realized that, obviously, Andy was not afraid of Luke Trull, and his respect for his partner increased. But he would not show himself as long as Luke was near.

Andy's search brought him very near, but Frosty remained perfectly still. His was the patience of a cat. Few other animals could wait so long or so uncomplainingly for exactly the right moment, be so sure of that moment when it arrived, and act accordingly. But one mistake was one too

many, and he had no intention of making any more. Finally,
Andy went back in the direction from which they had come.
After an interval, Luke Trull rose to follow him.

Frosty stayed in hiding. He had no idea as to what was
happening here, or why his partner and Luke Trull should
be together in the swamp, and he did not give a thought to
possible danger for Andy. Frosty had accepted him as a
partner largely because he was strong.

Frosty moved only when he was sure both had gone.

He wanted to go back to the house and wait for Andy
there, but he did not return directly to the slough over
which Andy had carried him. Only when forced to do so
would he enter water, and he knew perfectly well that he
could not cross the slough. He must find his own trail.

Because he was in thick brush, he made no effort to hide
but he did remain wholly alert. Slowing when he emerged
from the brush into a grove of trees, he saw water sparkling.
He went cautiously forward.

He looked out on a relatively quiet section of the same
slough, and as he gazed, a big bass broke water and splashed
back in. A log floated against the bank on the other side, and
a sora teetered on it. In a little eddy given over to lily pads,
a heron balanced on one leg and waited with poised bill for
an unwary fish to venture near. Frosty slunk back into the
brush and slipped into another grove of trees.

Suddenly he halted in his tracks.

High in one of the trees, a tamarack, he had seen something move. Little more than a flicker, it was enough to
make him aware of an alien presence. Flattening himself, he
held perfectly still and searched. Presently he saw clearly the
thing that had moved. It was another great horned owl.
Twenty feet from the ground, it perched close to the trunk

of the gloomy tamarack and enjoyed a nap. Frosty remained where he was.

Experience had taught him what these great birds could do, and again he wanted to escape notice because, if it came to a battle, he was not sure he would win it. The great owls were strong and unbelievably ferocious, and a motion might bring this one down upon him. Never taking his eyes from it, Frosty decided exactly what he would do if the owl swooped at him. If possible, he would get back into the brush.

He heard Andy come back to resume the search, but again he dared not move. His friend went away.

Twilight draped its gray mantle over the swamp, and finally the owl took wing. Frosty still did not move, for the owl merely soared gracefully over the slough, dipped to pluck a swimming muskrat from the water and winged into a dead tree to devour its prey. Frosty slunk away.

In the tamarack, the owl had been an unknown factor. It might be hungry and it might not. Now it was known. Having the muskrat, it would eat. After eating, it would not be hungry. Therefore, the chances of its hunting anything else in the near future were small. Frosty resumed his search for a way out of the swamp.

A while later, he knew that there was none. He was on a little island which he could not possibly leave unless he wanted to swim, and he would not swim. Hungry, Frosty gave himself over to finding something to eat. He prowled back through the brush without discovering anything, and when hunger emboldened him, he stalked among the trees. He struck at and missed a rabbit that promptly jumped into and swam across the slough.

The small island had never supported much life anyway,

and the owl had been living on it and hunting every night for almost two weeks. Many of the island's furred inhabitants had already fallen to it, and whatever had escaped knew it was here. The mice and gophers that remained ventured from their burrows only when necessity forced them to do so.

Hearing a bird stir, Frosty marked the tree in which it roosted and made his way there. He climbed and was ten feet from the ground when the bird took wing and rattled off into the darkness. Frosty descended the tree. He took a stance before a mouse's burrow and waited. But the mouse did not emerge.

Dawn was breaking and Frosty was still hungry when he went back to look for the owl. He found it still in the dead tree. He settled down to watch, for once again the owl was an unknown factor. It had fed last night, but it might be in the mood to feed again and the kitten was of no mind to serve as its next dinner. If he knew where his enemy was, he would also know what it was doing. He watched the owl all day.

Again, with the coming of dusk, the owl winged out to get another muskrat. Little interested in the muskrats' fate and unable to catch one himself because none climbed out on the island, Frosty could not know that the owl had found a bonanza here. Its plan was to remain, with little need to exert itself, until it had caught every one of the ten muskrats Andy had planted. Then it would seek another hunting ground.

Knowing that once more it was safe to prowl, for the owl would not hunt until it was again hungry, Frosty knew also that he must have something to quiet his own raging hunger. But if he hunted frantically or hastily, he would frighten his prey instead of catching it. Returning to the mouse's den

he had watched last night, he settled himself down to wait. ....
Two hours later, the mouse poked a cautious nose out, then
came all the way from its burrow. Frosty pounced and
pinned his prey.

The mouse was a mere tidbit, but it eased the sharpest
hunger pangs. Frosty sought another burrow. He caught
nothing, and again with dawn he sought out the owl. It had
gone back to the tamarack and was almost hidden by the
tree's foliage. Following its customary routine, it went forth
at dusk to catch another muskrat, then winged into the dead
tree.

In the hope that the owl might have dropped some part
of its meal, Frosty nosed beneath the tamarack. He found
only furry pellets; such parts as the owl hadn't eaten were
cached in the tamarack's upper branches and Frosty did not
dare climb the tree because the dead stub in which the owl
perched was too near. Desperately, the kitten sought out
another mouse's burrow, but when he found one, he shed
his desperation and gave way to patience. He caught and ate
the mouse.

Seeking another burrow, he was thwarted when the gentle
wind that always murmured over the swamp became a stiff
breeze. He could not possibly hold still, for the wind ruffled
his fur and the mouse knew he waited.

Frosty prowled after daybreak. He knew he was taking
a chance, but it was not a great one, for so far the owl had
hunted only at twilight. When a crow cawed, the kitten
swung at once toward the sound. The crow was across the
slough and thus out of reach, but perhaps it would come
nearer and it offered the only present chance to get food.

Coming out on that quiet part of the slough where he had
seen the log, Frosty discovered that last night's stiff wind had

moved it. Now, instead of lying against the bank, it angled out into the water, with its nearer end only two feet away and its farther against the opposite bank. Seeing opportunity, Frosty seized it.

He sprang, landed on the log, ran swiftly across and leaped into tall swamp grass on the other side. Crossing the log had been a very dangerous moment for he was completely exposed while doing so. Now he was safe, and since peril was behind him, it could be forgotten. Frosty resumed stalking the crow.

He found it beside a branch of the slough, pecking at a small dead fish that had washed up there and calling at intervals. Frosty slunk through some tall grass and came to a place where foliage grew only in scattered places. He stopped to study the situation.

When the crow lowered its head to peck at the fish, he glided swiftly forward and hid behind a tuft of grass. He waited quietly when the bird looked around and glided to another tuft when it resumed feeding. Suddenly the crow saw him.

With a startled squawk, it beat frantically into the air, struggled to gain altitude and cawed derisively after it had done so. Frosty ran forward to get what was left of the little fish and the crow jeered at him again.

Winging over the kitten, presently the crow saw the owl in the dead tree and its raucous insults became a sharp, clear call. Another crow answered, and another. The owl was their enemy by night, when it came on silent wings to pluck sleeping crows from their roosts, but they were its masters by day.

The flock gathered and advanced to the attack. Diving on

the owl, they pecked with sharp beaks and beat with their wings. At first the owl fought back, but they were too many and too swift. Followed by the screaming crows, he winged across the swamp. The pursuit and the noise attending it died in the distance.

Lacking the faintest notion that, however indirectly, he had saved this colony of muskrats for Andy, Frosty finished his fish and went to hunt gophers.

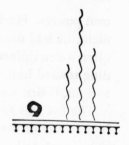

9

INTRUDER

Safely off the island, Frosty's main concern was something to eat. He set his course for the little knoll upon which he had discovered the gopher colony.

While remaining aware of everything about him, he walked more openly than he ever had before and far more confidently. Bigger than average from birth, he was fulfilling his early promise of becoming an unusually large cat. Traces of the kitten remained, but his stride was almost that of an adult and great muscles were already prominent in his neck, front quarters and shoulders. The life he'd been forced to lead had developed them and, in advance of full maturity, had made him tough as rawhide. But though he had inherited his father's size, he also had his mother's grace and balanced proportions. Frosty was big without being even slightly awkward.

He walked more freely because, with increasing size and experience, there had come an increasing awareness of his

119

own powers. Having killed a rattlesnake and put a coyote to flight, he had discovered for himself that the best defense is often a determined offense. So when he saw a gray fox padding toward him, instead of running or hiding, he prepared to fight, if that were necessary.

The fox was an old and wise veteran that had been born in a corner of the swamp, had hunted in it since he'd been old enough to hunt, and that knew its every corner. He had a mate and cubs that had left their hillside den a couple of weeks ago, and last night he'd gone hunting with his family. But the cubs were still clumsy hunters who frightened more game than they caught, and the two baby muskrats that the old fox had finally snatched had been just enough to satisfy them. Hunting for herself, the fox's mate had had several mice and a woodcock.

The dog fox had eaten nothing. Now, while his lazy family rested in a thicket, he was out to find a meal for himself.

He walked openly, depending on his nose to guide him to food, because he knew and did not fear the swamp. Since attaining full growth, the only natural enemies that had ever challenged him were occasional coyotes, and if the fox did not choose to run from them, or fight, he could always climb a tree. Andy Gates was the only human being who ever penetrated very deeply into the swamp, and Andy was confined to certain paths and trails which the fox did not have to travel. However, his nose had already told him that Andy was not in the swamp today.

The muskrats were new to the swamp. Yet, to the experienced fox, they were an old story. Among any young animals, there were always a certain number of unwise or incautious. They seldom lasted long, but after catching the pair of youngsters, the fox had wasted no time hunting more because all the others had stayed out of reach in the water.

He was on his way to a rabbit colony of which he knew when Frosty's scent crossed his nostrils. He stopped at once, knowing it for an alien scent; then followed his nose toward it. Six feet away, he stopped again.

Frosty's jaws framed a snarl, and a warning growl rumbled in his chest. Every hair on his body was fluffed, making him seem twice his actual size. His tail was stiffly erect and fluffed, too, and his muscles were ready to carry him into battle. For a moment the fox regarded him closely, then circled and trotted on. The fox was wise enough to know that Frosty did not merely look dangerous. He was dangerous.

Frosty resumed his own course toward the gopher colony. He remembered it to the last detail, and he had not forgotten the rattlesnake that lived there. The snake was still present, but it had recently fed and was sluggish. Frosty settled himself in front of a gopher's den.

He held perfectly still, eyes fixed on the burrow's mouth, and presently, deep in the earth, he heard a gopher moving. He remained quiet until the little rodent emerged from its den, then pounced. He caught his prey, devoured it and made a half-hearted pass at the snake. But he did not continue the battle because he was anxious to see Andy, and, now that he had eaten, he could go find his partner. Frosty made his way toward the house.

He knew before he emerged from the swamp that Andy was not there. Though the kitten lacked a keen sense of smell, wood smoke had a pungent odor that lingered for a long time, and there had been no recent fire in the stove. Frosty came out of the swamp to see the persistent doe, that had not yet given up hope of getting into the garden, resting beside it. A crow sat on the house's ridgepole and croaked raucous insults to the four winds. Scurrying across the porch, a striped chipmunk dived into a crevice. Frosty marked him down; the gopher had not filled his stomach.

As soon as he climbed onto the porch, he knew that the house had been unoccupied for several days. It had a cold and deserted air, like a frame from which the picture had been removed, and the odors that seeped under the door were cold ones. Frosty cried his loneliness, but he did not question his friend's absence. He reserved for himself the right to go prowling and to stay for as long as it suited him. It naturally followed that Andy had the same privilege, and sooner or later he would come back.

Frosty settled beside the crevice in which the chipmunk had disappeared. He caught the furry little animal, ate it, and his hunger was satisfied. Curling up in his favorite place, he settled himself for a nap. All about were familiar things, and even while he napped, his ears brought him their story. He heard the doe rise and begin to crop grass, birds crying in the swamp, the murmur of the wind, muskrats swimming in the slough, and he awakened to none of it because it was familiar. But an hour later, when he heard a man walking, he glided silently under the porch and waited there. He'd heard those footsteps before, and he knew who was coming.

Five minutes later, Luke Trull passed the house and went into the swamp. Frosty watched with anger in his eyes, knowing only that once again he had been near his deadliest enemy. He couldn't possibly know that Luke wouldn't have dared let himself be seen going into the swamp, or even past the house, had Andy been home. Nor could Frosty understand, as Luke did, that Andy was in jail and would not be back for several days.

Luke disappeared in the tall swamp grass. He knew where Andy had planted his twenty pairs of muskrats and the safe trails to them, for Andy himself had inadvertently pointed them out. Luke did not know how many other colonies there were or their locations, but there would never be a safer time to look for them. He had his own plans, and he had already decided how and when he intended to strike. All he had to find out was where.

Evening shadows were long when hunger forced Frosty from the house. He left reluctantly, for he was very lonesome and ached for Andy's presence, but he must have food. The kitten stalked down to the slough in which Four-Leaf and Clover were making their home. Only two of the young remained, and they had built themselves a very clumsy house at the slough's far end. The others—partly spurred by a natural wanderlust of youth and partly driven by irritable parents that were expecting new babies and had no time for the old—had gone into the swamp.

Frosty flattened himself, and again anger flared in his eyes. Luke Trull came back out of the swamp and took himself off toward the road. Waiting until the hated man was out of hearing, Frosty went on.

He stalked a red-winged blackbird that was swaying on a reed, sprang—and lashed his tail in anger when the bird escaped him. He glared after the bird as it flew, knowing that he should have made a kill and not understanding why he had not. He leaped at a mouse that was moving through its grass-thatched tunnel and missed by a fraction of an inch. Twenty minutes later, he missed a strike at a woodcock that whistled away in front of him.

Chagrined by these failures, Frosty went deeper into the swamp. His hunger grew, but so did his bad luck. For some

reason, everything in the swamp seemed to be not only unusually alert but extraordinarily agile. Frosty missed five
more strikes at mice and three at various birds. Casting
back and forth, he sought for new quarry.

Black night found him deep in the swamp and still hungry.
Hearing fresh game, he broke into a swift run. But again his
luck was bad.

He'd heard a young muskrat, one of the sons of Four-Leaf
and Clover, swimming up a thin finger of water that led
over a little knob and into a slough. The kitten reached the
knob a split second after the youngster jumped into the
slough and swam away. Twitching an angry tail and glaring,
Frosty watched the little drama that unfolded before him.

Another young muskrat, a daughter of the cautious pair,
was already in the slough. The two met, looked awkwardly
at each other, swam in circles, then climbed out on a half-
submerged log and became better acquainted. Finally, side
by side, they dived beneath an overhanging bank and began
to enlarge a burrow that the little female had already started.
They were simply two lonely, lost youngsters who, for the
present, were happy just to have each other's company. But
if both lived, next year there would be another muskrat
colony.

Frosty stalked and missed a rabbit, and made a wild spring
at a grouse that was roosting in the lower branches of a
tamarack. When the grouse rattled off in the darkness, he
spat. Then he regained his self-control. Irritated by repeated failures, he had been striking furiously but wildly,
and that was no way to hunt. He must follow a careful plan.

When he heard deer grazing, he trotted toward them.
They were a little herd of two does with three fawns that
browsed together. A short distance from them a huge buck,

a craggy-horned old patriarch of the swamp, kept to himself, but from time to time cast possessive glances at the does. Still farther away, where he could flee into the swamp if the bigger one chased him, a smaller buck grazed nervously. The big buck and the small one had spent a companionable winter, spring and part of the summer in a secluded thicket. Now, though the rutting season was still weeks away, both were becoming interested in the does and jealousy had come between them.

The big buck raised his head, shook his antlers and stamped a threatening hoof when Frosty came near. The kitten looked haughtily at him. He'd known deer for a long while, and he could elude any charge they made. He waited patiently near the does and fawns, and when they disturbed a mouse that leaped in panic-stricken haste from them, he caught and ate it. Trotting to overtake the grazing deer, he caught the next mouse they disturbed and the one after that. His hunger satisfied, he cleaned himself thoroughly and started back toward the house. Thus, the first hunting trick he had ever learned again proved valuable.

The house was still cold, and the odors seeping under the door were stale ones. Again, Frosty cried his loneliness. Then he settled himself on the porch to wait and hope for Andy's return.

For the following three days, Luke Trull went into the swamp every morning and stayed until evening. His trespassing enraged the kitten, not because the man trespassed but because he was an enemy who came near. If Frosty had known how, he would have worked some harm on Luke. But he did not know how. It would be the sheerest folly to attack a man unless every advantage was on his own side,

so he hid when Luke passed and again when the hillman emerged from the swamp.

Then Luke appeared no more. Frosty's concerns narrowed to keeping his belly filled and waiting anxiously for Andy's return.

Andy, serving his ten days in the town jail with nothing whatever to do, had ample time to think. And the more he thought, the more evident it became that he had walked squarely into a cunning trap. It was none of the young Trooper's doing. That embarrassed youngster had visited Andy and explained that, usually, in such cases, Justice Benton levied a small fine and a big lecture. Benton himself might be pardoned partly on the grounds of his own ignorance and partly because of a social system which, for political expediency, gave a man of his caliber wide and flexible authority.

Luke Trull, and Luke alone, had set the trap, baited it, lured his victim—and sprung his trap when the time was ripe. Andy figured out to his own satisfaction exactly why things could have turned out no other way.

A townsman, brought before Justice Benton on a minor assault charge, probably would have been let off with a fine and a lecture. But in the town's opinion, which meant majority opinion, there was a vast difference between town and hill dwellers. The former were commonly supposed to be law-abiding. The latter were not only generally considered lawless, but they were also a different breed of people who merited different treatment. A townsman could understand the law A hillman could better understand jail, and that was a state of affairs which Luke Trull comprehended to perfection.

Aside from being aware that there was a very good chance of Andy's serving a jail sentence, Luke had also known that he would be ordered to keep the peace. If he appeared again on an assault charge, his sentence might very well be six months instead of ten days.

Lying on his bunk and staring at the ceiling, Andy conceded that he had been stupid as a fox cub just learning to hunt. It was, he decided, not only possible but probable that Luke, knowing the boy would resort to violence, had exposed himself deliberately. It was another tribute to his cunning that he had not let himself be seen until after he discovered where Andy put the last of his twenty pairs of muskrats.

Andy grinned ruefully and thought of Joe Wilson. He should have listened to the game warden, but he hadn't listened and here he was. However, there were still some puzzling aspects to the situation.

If Andy's fondest hopes were realized, and there were 200 muskrats in the swamp by spring, they would still represent no fortune. It was hard to believe that even Luke Trull would go to this much trouble for what the reward might be. On the other hand, Luke knew definitely only that Andy had planted at least the 20 pairs and some before that. He did not know how many had been previously planted, and he might think there were a great many more than actually had been liberated. Andy narrowed his eyes.

Luke, nobody's fool, would not trap furs in the summer because they were worthless then, and he was not one to exert himself for nothing. So, except for those that fell to natural predators, the muskrats were safe during Andy's sojourn in jail. But Luke could and probably would take advantage of Andy's absence to explore the swamp and locate as many other colonies as possible.

The jail's outer door opened. The waiter from a cafe across the street brought Andy's supper and handed it through the cell bars. Ordinarily aloof, tonight the fellow was talkative.

"Here you are, Bud."

Andy said, "Thanks."

"What are you in for?" the waiter asked.

"I murdered my grandmother."

The waiter grinned. "They say you guys from the hills do take pot shots at each other."

"We have to have some entertainment."

"How many more days you got?"

"After tomorrow, I'll no longer be a guest here."

"They say," the waiter pursued his interrogation, "that you and another guy fought over some muskrats?"

"For once," Andy agreed, "rumor got something right."

"Really?"

"Really."

"And you're in jail on account of some muskrats?"

"That's right."

The waiter continued, "I've heard that it's as much as a man's life is worth to go into those hills alone at night."

"Oh, don't talk like a fool!" Andy snapped.

"I was just being civil," the waiter retorted sulkily.

The man left and Andy was alone with his dinner and his thoughts. He nibbled listlessly at the food. The waiter exemplified the town's attitude; hillmen would fight over anything, even worthless muskrats in a worthless swamp. In their opinion, it was a small thing, and not a project upon which a man hoped to build a career and a life.

Out of the dim past, ghosts came to haunt Andy. He saw again the men of the Gates clan, the older men who had asked neither favors nor assistance from anyone. They had settled their own problems in their own way or died trying, and if they died, no survivor had ever looked to the law for redress.

Andy forced the ghosts from his mind. Their ways had suited their times, but there were different times. Nobody could be his own law, and taking the law into one's own hands could lead only to disaster. Besides, the boy thought, he must not borrow trouble. Luke Trull had not yet raided his muskrats, and at least as much as anything else, his own hot-headedness was responsible for his present predicament. Andy went to sleep.

The next morning, two hours after breakfast, a State Policeman came to unlock the cell. It was not the young trooper but an older, hardened man who looked at Andy with no more personal interest than a scientist wastes on a specimen.

"Okeh." The trooper nodded toward the door. "You can go."

Andy walked through the open door, and from the cafe across the street two men stared curiously at him. He turned away, his face burning, and walked swiftly out of town. He had a sudden, vast need for the swamp and the things that were of the swamp. Somehow he felt that, when he was once again where he belonged, this would seem just another bad dream. He hurried along into the hills and when he came to the path leading to his place, half ran down it.

He was still a hundred yards from the house when Frosty came running happily to greet him. Andy stooped to caress his partner, and the kitten arched against his legs and purred. Side by side, they walked to the house.

Entering, Andy took his .22 from its rack, then the two partners went contentedly into the swamp.

10

ANDY HUNTS

A north wind, whistling across the swamp, launched a savage attack against Andy's house, broke in half and snarled fiercely around either side. Bearing a scattering of snowflakes, the wind whipped away the thin plume of smoke that curled from the chimney and whirled dry leaves across the yard. A little flock of sparrows that had gone to roost under the eaves fluffed their feathers, huddled close together for warmth and twittered sleepily of the lenient weather that had been. The doe that had tried all summer to get into Andy's garden walked through the open gate and happily crunched cabbage stalks from which the heads had been cut.

The doe raised her head. Chewing lustily, she stared into the wind-stirred night. Her ears flicked forward and her eyes were big with interest. Something was coming, but it was nothing to fear. A moment later, a buck came out of the swamp.

It was the smaller of the two bucks Frosty had seen when

133

he waited for the deer to frighten mice toward him. There was a bloody welt along his flank and he limped slightly with his right front leg. When the right time came, he had fought the old patriarch for the two does and had been defeated by the bigger, stronger buck. But there was no denying the season or the forces that drove him.

The doe came out of the garden, and the pair halted, ten feet apart. Then, with mincing little steps, they closed the distance between them. The buck arched his swollen neck, shook his antlers and pawed the ground. Stepping high, like a parade horse, he danced clear around the doe and nudged her gently. The doe brushed his flank with her black muzzle and, after five minutes, they went into the hills together. The big buck, who would not be averse to adding another wife to his harem, waited in the swamp.

High over the swamp, a V-line of wild geese let themselves be tumbled along by the wind. At a signal from their leader, they banked, glided into the swamp and settled in the center of a pond. With morning, when they could see any enemies that might be lurking on the bank, they would go to feed.

Three young muskrats, a male and two females, that had been busy cutting reeds and taking them into a roomy burrow, dived in panicky haste when the geese alighted. After a while, screening themselves beneath some frozen rushes that overhung the bank, they came up to see what was happening. When the geese did not make any hostile moves, they resumed cutting and storing reeds.

In the middle branches of a tamarack that had shed its needles, a great horned owl ripped at a muskrat which it had plucked from a slough's surface. Another owl, on the way to hunt, floated silently past.

Mice stayed deep in their burrows and stirred only when

it was necessary to gather seeds to eat. Gophers did not move at all, and rattlesnakes had long since sought winter dens in which the frost could not touch them. As though knowing it was well to eat as much as possible while there was still plenty to be had, a rabbit stuffed itself. A lithe mink that had just swum a slough pointed its snake-like head at the rabbit, stalked, pounced and made a kill.

In the house, Andy slept snugly and soundly beneath warm quilts. Frosty was curled beside him. . . . So the night passed.

Andy awakened when the first gray light of an autumn morning was just beginning to play with the black windows. His hand stole to Frosty, who pushed a furry head against it and licked his partner's palm with a raspy tongue. For a few extra minutes, Andy listened to the snarling wind and enjoyed the comfort of his bed. He had a sense of well-being which the bitter weather to be served only to intensify.

Sometimes alone and sometimes with Frosty—and always carrying his .22, the shells for which were inexpensive—he had been in the swamp every day. More muskrats had been lost and that he knew, but on the whole, they had done better than he thought they could. Prowling every slough and every arm of every slough that he was able to reach and carefully watching every pond, he had found sixty-one different colonies. Each contained at least a pair, for the older muskrats that had lost their mates had traveled until they had found others. Some adults had taken young mates, and some of the older males had fought savagely for theirs. There were colonies which Andy knew definitely contained at least three muskrats, and there was one with five.

In addition, and despite the fact that he had searched as thoroughly as he could, there was a distinct possibility that he had not located every colony. Some of the sloughs had so many arms and branches that they were practically water systems within themselves, and some of the branches were hidden by foliage. With luck, there should be at least 200 muskrats by spring, and that was one reason why the north wind sang such a beautiful song.

Andy had shot another great horned owl. He had caught another fox and a bobcat, which he knew were raiding his muskrats, and this in a time of plenty, when anything with more than mediocre hunting skill could fill its belly. Now the migratory birds were going or had already gone. Soon mice would be moving beneath snow, rather than grass tunnels. That left little except grouse, which were very wise and very hard to catch; sparrows, chickadees and the few other birds that stayed throughout the winter; and rabbits.

However, predators did not migrate. The hungry season, which would bring fierce competition for available food, was just around the corner. But ice-locked ponds and sloughs would protect the muskrats from almost everything. If Andy could see his charges through the next four to six weeks, he should be able to bring most of them safely through the winter. Of course, there was always a possibility of bitter cold that would freeze shallow ponds and sloughs to the bottom. If any water did freeze in such a fashion, muskrats trapped there would starve, merely because they had to be able to move about in order to get food. But most of the colonies were in water deep enough to be safe, regardless of what the weather brought, and only about one winter in ten was very severe.

Andy had a sobering thought. No ice would deter Luke Trull, the deadliest predator of all! Andy had expected the fellow to strike before this. Though far from their best, soon pelts would be good enough to command a fair price. However, Luke had not come and Andy hoped he would not.

Frosty rose, stretched, leaped lightly to the floor and delivered himself of a querulous call. Andy grinned and sat up in bed.

"Time to be moving, huh?"

He swung out of bed, padded across the floor, lifted the stove lid, stirred the gray ashes with his lid lifter and dropped dry kindling on hot coals. Fire nibbled anxiously at the kindling, then took a big bite and flame crackled. Andy dressed. He lifted the lid again to add some chunks of wood and looked out the window.

The wind still blew hard; but after spitting out just enough snow to dust everything, rolling black clouds had closed their mouths tightly. The thermometer outside the window registered exactly one degree above freezing. Andy cut slices from a slab of bacon and laid them in a skillet. His eyes were questioning and he strained to listen. This first real touch of winter should have brought more than just a north wind; wild geese should have blown in, too. But he could not hear them calling.

Frosty looked expectantly at his partner, voiced an imperious command and walked to the door. Andy let him out. Frosty had had no breakfast, but that was nothing to worry about. No longer a kitten but a great cat, he was well able to take care of himself and Andy had long since discovered that, though he made no distinction between young and old, or male and female, he did not kill wantonly. He did take what he wanted to satisfy his hunger, but so did everything else. Andy broke eggs into the skillet and laid two slices of bread on the stove to toast.

He was always busy, but during the next six weeks he'd

be doubly so. With waterfowl season open, small game season about to open, and deer hunting to follow that, the time had arrived both to enjoy sport and to fill his winter larder. Andy hurried through breakfast and the morning's housework, took a double-barreled twelve gauge shotgun from the gun rack, pulled his boots on and donned a wool jacket. He thrust half a dozen number two shells into his pocket and went into the swamp.

He walked fast, paying little attention to the noise he made and making no special effort to conceal himself. Geese were the wariest of game, and only by accident would a flock alight on any accessible pond or slough. They preferred hidden places, deep in the swamp, and long experience had taught Andy where to find waters which the geese liked best.

The boy halted to watch a couple of young muskrats that were frantically cutting reeds to store for winter use. He shook his head in wonder. These animals were the offspring of some muskrats he had liberated. They'd never faced a winter in the swamp; they hadn't even lived through a winter, but they still knew enough to cut and store food. How did they know? Andy couldn't explain it, nor could anyone else. Instinct, perhaps, was responsible for part, but Andy had never accepted the theory that instinct is responsible for all a wild creature's actions. If this were true, the muskrats he had planted should have known by instinct that there would be predators about. They'd had to learn, but in learning, they had passed some knowledge on to their offspring. The young were more wary than their parents had been. Maybe, Andy thought, only the fittest of the adults he'd planted had survived. They'd lived because they were smarter or stronger, or perhaps both. It followed that most of the offspring of such parents would be smart and strong too, and thus it became a process of natural selection.

He went on and came to a long, wide slough in which the five muskrats lived. Relatively shallow, the slough had a quicksand bottom, and, according to legend, the bones of two men lay somewhere in its depths. They were a Gates and a Trull who had met here, started a hand-to-hand battle and tumbled into the water. In this instance, legend probably was strictly fancy, with no basis in fact. The slough was not deep, but a good swimmer who knew what he was doing might have every chance of crossing it safely. Andy frowned.

On the far side of the slough was a high knob. A scattering of brush and scrub aspen grew there, and almost at the very edge of the slough was a huge sycamore with gnarled branches and a hollow trunk. A well-marked path led out of the water into the hollow.

Andy's frown deepened. Muskrats had made the path, and if they intended to live in the hollow sycamore, they risked a very precarious situation. Predators could reach them there, but, above and beyond that danger, they'd be locked out of the slough when it froze. Then, even if they did not fall to some fanged or taloned prowler, they'd starve. Muskrats could not live on hard-frozen vegetation.

Andy went around the slough, broke his shotgun and extracted the shells, then leaned his weapon against an aspen. He knelt beside the sycamore, but when he sought to support himself with his left hand, he slipped and his arm sank to the elbow in mud. Scrambling hastily to pull himself back, he grimaced at the muddy sleeve, cleaned it as best he could with a handful of rushes and removed his jacket to wring the water out. It was not yet cold enough to make it necessary to start a fire so he might dry out the jacket.

The next time he knelt, he braced his left hand against the sycamore before he peered into the gloomy interior. When his eyes became adjusted to the darkness, he saw a burrow at the far end. Satisfied, he rose. The muskrats were not naturally lazy creatures that had chosen to live in the sycamore, rather than dig their own den. They were merely using the hollow as a partial shelter for a surface den, and doubtless there was another exit that led directly into the water. Andy searched until he found it, under an overhanging bank.

He caught up his shotgun, reloaded and continued into the swamp. A hundred yards farther on, a young deer, a spring-born fawn, looked steadily at him, twitched long ears, stamped a nervous hoof, then hoisted a white tail and bounded into the swamp. It was followed by two more fawns, which, in turn, were trailed by a pair of adult does. Andy stood perfectly still. At this season, a buck should be with the does and he wanted to locate the buck.

After a moment, he saw what he was looking for. Off in the swamp grass was the barest ripple of motion, a phantom thing that at first seemed not even to exist. It was the craggy-horned old patriarch, the same beast that Frosty had seen and that, later, had driven his smaller rival away. Too smart to show himself in any open space, the old buck was sneaking, almost unseen, through grass that was tall enough to cover his back. But he had forgotten about his antlers, and now and again they showed. Andy watched closely until the old buck was out of sight.

Every year, if for nothing except for winter meat, a buck was a necessity and this was far and away the biggest in the swamp. But he was also by far the wisest. Andy had hunted him for the past three seasons and had managed only a couple of snap shots at him. The old buck refused to be driven from the swamp, and he was acquainted with every inch of that. He never panicked, seldom made an unwise move, and he knew all about hunters with firearms.

Andy bent his head against the wind and walked on. Four weeks would bring another deer season and he intended to spend at least the first half of it matching wits with the old patriarch. If he couldn't get him, he'd take a smaller buck. He looked again at the rolling black clouds.

He had heard no geese nor had he seen any, but it was goose weather and they should be down. Nearing the slough where he hoped to find them, Andy crouched so that his head was below the tops of the swamp grass. He knew the game he sought. Not even the old buck was warier or harder to approach. When the boy saw the tops of some tamaracks that flanked the slough, he held the shotgun in his right hand and crawled. He advanced with almost painful slowness. A suspicious sound could warn geese as swiftly as an enemy in sight. The last twenty yards Andy wriggled on his stomach. He looked through a fringe of swamp grass at the slough.

More than twenty geese swam on it, but the sentry they'd posted had become suspicious and had alerted the others. Positive that the geese had not seen him, and until now equally certain that they had not heard him, Andy grinned his appreciation. He must have made some sound which possibly nothing except a wild goose could have detected, but his stalk was successful. Well within range, all he had to do was stand up and get two of the flock when they took to the air. Then his glance strayed across the slough and he muttered under his breath.

One on a lower branch and one on an upper, two great horned owls sat in the same tamarack. Andy muttered again.

Within easy range of wild geese, he might have at least two. But choosing them meant letting the owls go, and if he did, he might very well pay for his choice with a dozen or more muskrats. Andy sighed.

He leveled his shotgun, sighted on the topmost owl and squeezed the trigger. Almost before the booming report died, he got the second owl with the other barrel. In a frantic haste, he ejected the two empty shells and slipped fresh ones in, but with a great flapping of wings, the geese were already airborne. Andy sighed again and watched them go. He still might shoot, but he could no longer be certain of a kill and it was far better to let the geese escape than to wound one.

Andy turned dejectedly away from the slough. His swamp was not on one of the great flyways, down or up which, according to the season, waterfowl stream. Only the strays alighted here, and some seasons they were very few. The boy shrugged and walked on. The two geese he had hoped to get would have provided his Christmas and Thanksgiving dinners—and several more besides. But the great horned owls were far too dangerous to be tolerated. Andy longed for the freeze-up that would make his muskrats safe.

The next day, on a different slough, Andy bagged two mallards out of a flock that beat hastily into the air before him, and the day after that he got two more. He plucked and dressed the ducks, wrapped each separately in flour sacking and hung it in his shed to freeze. These were the last of the waterfowl. If more came, he missed them.

The weather, never very cold or very warm, dropped to a few degrees below freezing every night and climbed a few degrees above it every day. There were some more snow flurries and brittle shell ice formed on the edges of some ponds and sloughs. But, except in places that were shadowed all day long, both snow and ice melted under the noon sun. Andy made ready for the trapping and small game season.

An hour before dawn on opening day, he had breakfasted. He let Frosty out, and with the shotgun under his arm, started off.

His way led him into the hills, rather than the swamp, for this morning he intended to set fox traps and there were more foxes in the hills. Black night was just shading into gray dawn when he threaded his path among a copse of scrub oak toward a huge stump that had supported a great pine but that was now a melancholy, moss- and lichen-covered relic. Andy pawed aside some dead leaves that seemed to have blown into the stump and revealed his fox traps.

Along with a packsack, leather trapping gloves, a roll of canvas, a bottle of scent, trap stakes and even the hatchet used to drive the stakes, they had been in the stump all summer and no trace of human scent could possibly cling to them. Before doing anything else, Andy slipped his hands into the gloves. Being careful to touch them with nothing except the gloves, he put eight traps, eight stakes, the roll of canvas, the hatchet and the bottle of scent into the packsack and shouldered it. The hills were cut with numerous tote roads over which, at one time, wagons loaded with timber had traveled. Though some were brush-grown, most such roads remained open enough so that foxes en route from one place to another traveled them. Approaching such a road, Andy stopped.

He unrolled his strip of canvas, walking on it as he did so. When he came to the middle of the road, he knelt to study the ground carefully. After he was sure he had memorized every tiny detail, he used the hatchet's blade to scoop a hole just big enough to hide a set trap. The surplus earth he scattered to either side. He started a stake through the trap ring and kept pounding until the top of the stake was level with its surroundings. Then he replaced every leaf and every blade of grass exactly as it had been.

Andy took the bottle of scent from his pack, uncorked it and grimaced. The scent was a nauseous substance, composed of exactly measured portions of thoroughly rotted fish; the castor, or scent glands, of beaver; oil of asafetida and oil of wintergreen. Its odor would shame the most formidable skunk, but foxes found it irresistible! Andy put one drop on his set trap and, rolling up his canvas as he did so, walked backwards. In like manner, he set seven more fox traps.

He hurried back toward the house, for he wanted to spend the afternoon in his swamp, but when a fat rabbit with a flashing white tail scooted before him, he shot it. He collected four more rabbits, the bag limit for one day. However, the possession limit was ten and rabbits were plentiful. If he froze these five and four more, he would still have one under the possession limit and, whenever he felt so inclined, he would be entitled to shoot a rabbit for his dinner. Andy skinned and dressed his rabbits and hung them in the shed. After a hurried lunch, he exchanged his pacs for boots and went into the swamp with mink traps.

After reading sign in the few snows that had lingered after sunup, he had determined that there were sixteen mink in the swamp. If he took ten, there would still be enough to perform the necessary functions of such predators, such as catching sick rabbits that would otherwise spread disease and restocking the swamp next year.

Andy waded a winding little watercourse. He knew mink as inquisitive creatures that will investigate and, if possible, squeeze into every crack and crevice along their line of travel. On this knowledge he had based his plan for trapping mink without catching any muskrats, which also might travel the waterways. He set his traps at places which mink would investigate but muskrats were likely to avoid, and he baited each with a tiny bit of scent from the scent glands of mink trapped last year. On the way home, he shot two grouse and added them to his collection in the shed.

Thereafter, while the weather became neither very cold nor unduly warm, Andy went into the hills every morning and into the swamp every afternoon. He added lustrous fox pelts to his cache in the fur shed, took the ten mink he wanted to catch in eight days and worried because the winter freeze was late. However, neither Luke Trull nor any extraordinary wave of natural predators had as yet attacked the muskrat colonies.

The night before deer season opened, Andy took his 30-30 from its rack and looked through the spotless bore. He put the rifle to his shoulder, squinted over the sights, and in imagination he was actually sighting on the great swamp buck.

The next morning, he set out on what he was sure would be the hardest hunt of his life.

At first Frosty was puzzled by and resentful of the strange madness that had suddenly come over his partner. He had gone once with Andy into the swamp and once into the hills, and each time his companion had used his shotgun. Though Frosty did not mind the snap of a .22, the blast of this great weapon was a tremendous shock to feline nerves. After the first discharge, he'd hoped that Andy would never fire the shotgun again. After the second, he decided definitely that

he would not be around if it were shot off any more. Thereafter, when Andy carried the shotgun, and he carried it every
day, Frosty took himself elsewhere.

Angry at first, feline philosophy came to Frosty's aid. It
was decidedly a madness—anyone who would make such a
noise had to be insane—but sooner or later Andy would
regain his senses and they could take up their companionship
where it had been broken off. Frosty roamed the swamp,
going where he wished and doing as he pleased, for he was
very sure of himself and his own powers now.

The night before deer season opened, he fed heartily on a
rabbit, slept in a hollow log . . . and resumed prowling. Just
before daylight, he came upon the big buck.

The fawns had long since been driven away to shift for
themselves and one of the does had gone of her own free will.
When the patriarch approached the remaining doe, she
slashed viciously at him with a front hoof and ran a few
steps. The second time he came near, she slashed again and
disappeared in the swamp grass. Still in the grip of the rutting season's urge, the angry buck scraped the ground with
his antlers.

Frosty watched with interest. He had never met his superior. Except for Andy, he had never even met his equal, so
he understood this enraged beast. The cat soft-footed to an
aspen that grew in front of a ledge of rocks and gauged the
exact distance to a crevice beneath the ledge. Then he
deliberately showed himself. At once the buck charged.

Frosty scrambled up the aspen and looked down contemptuously as the great creature raked the tree with his antlers,
snorted and fell to scraping the earth with a front hoof. He
reared—a move Frosty had anticipated—and the black cat dug
his nose with a single lightning-like thrust of his paw. Then

he leaped out of the tree and, with the buck pounding behind him, dodged into the crevice.

Snorting and puffing, the buck stamped angrily back and forth. He stopped and tried to edge an antler into the crevice. When his nose came near enough, Frosty scratched it again. The buck, all fury, thought only of reaching and killing this insignificant thing that had dared defy him.

For a time Frosty amused himself by scratching the patriarch's nose every time it came within reach. Then he withdrew to the rear of the crevice and went to sleep. The buck could not reach him, and while the furious beast stood guard, nothing else would try. Frosty slept peacefully, wholly at ease.

Daylight had bloomed when he was awakened by footsteps. From their rhythm and cadence, he knew they were Andy's. The cat waited. He'd be happy to meet his partner again, providing Andy had left the shotgun home.

Then came a blast that outdid even the shotgun's and Frosty crouched very quietly in his crevice. Andy was still mad, the cat decided, for he was still going about making noises that could not possibly be tolerated by anything in its right mind. However, the buck had hit the ground very hard and very suddenly, and now it lay very still. Frosty heard Andy's amazed,

"I'll be dog-goned! Hunt *this* buck for three years and then stumble right over him! Wonder how he got his nose dug that way?"

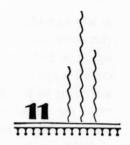

11

THE WAR OF THE OWLS

The next morning, knife in hand, Andy knelt beside his big buck and expertly skinned out both hindquarters. Frosty, entirely at ease as long as no rifles or shotguns were about, sat contentedly near and watched the proceedings with interest. Slitting the tendons, Andy tied a rope through each, slung the other ends of the ropes over a porch beam and made ready to hoist the carcass aloft and finish skinning.

Frosty slipped into his favorite hiding place under the porch and did not come out again. Andy slackened the taut ropes and eased the buck down onto the floor. Frosty was not precisely a watch dog, but the boy had learned to tell from the big cat's actions when something was coming.

A little while later, Jud Casman appeared around a corner of the house. He was dressed for hunting, but not precisely in the costume which fashion magazines say the well-dressed hunter should wear. He wore wool trousers whose legs had been slit so that they might fit over knee-length rubber boots.

149

It was a good, practical arrangement; snow and water would run down the trouser legs, rather than inside the boots. His upper torso was encased in a jacket over which he wore the cut-off upper half of some red woolen underwear. That, according to Jud, both enabled other hunters to see him and made the jacket snug enough so that some loose end wasn't forever catching in the brush. His hat might have descended to Jud from the first person ever to see the swamp. His rifle matched the costume.

It was a muzzle-loader of a type generally associated with frontiersmen and Indian fighters, and it was almost as long as Jud was tall. A single shot, it had been handed down by Jud's father, who in turn had obtained it from his father. The bore had been re-reamed and re-rifled so many times that now it cast a slug approximately the size of a small cannon ball. A lot of people had laughed at Jud and his rifle, but on his side, Jud snickered at those who needed a whole handful of cartridges when, as any child should know, one ball was plenty, if you put it in the right place. Andy, who had seen Jud pick the heads off squirrels and grouse and shoot flying geese, knew that Jud killed whatever he shot at. He left no wounded creature to die in agony.

Jud eyed the big buck and expressed his opinion, *"Hm-m."*

Andy said, "It's the big one."

"Give ya a heap of trouble?"

"I walked right up to him," Andy admitted. "He didn't even run."

"I'll give ya a hand," Jud offered. "Just snug them ropes when I lift."

Jud leaned his rifle against the house. No big man, he lifted the 200-pound buck without visible strain or effort and Andy tightened the ropes. Saying not another word, Jud picked up his rifle and went into the swamp.

Andy resumed his work, cutting with the knife point and pulling the loosened skin down around the carcass. Since this was deer season, obviously Jud was going into the swamp to get himself a deer. Andy knew where there were some, but if Jud had wanted advice, he'd have asked for it. Andy skinned his buck down and severed the head as close to the scalp as possible.

He grinned. Some years ago, Old Man Haroldson had taken a party deer hunting and among them they had shot five deer. When it came time to divide the venison, the hunters, with visions of choice steaks and roasts, had offered Old Man Haroldson the five necks. He had accepted with alacrity, and ever since had been gleefully telling how he put one over on the city-slickers, for the neck was the best part of any deer, in his opinion. Whether it was or not, Andy thought, there was a lot of good meat in it.

Frosty came out from beneath the porch and again sat companionably close. He turned up his nose at a little chunk of venison Andy threw him. Able to take his choice of the finest viands in the swamp, Frosty would accept second best only when he could not get first.

Andy looked with regret at the great antlers, a really fine trophy. But it cost money to have a deer head mounted, and he had no money to spare. He consoled himself with the thought that the antlers, sawed from the scalp and nailed over his door, would still look very nice. He split the carcass and made ready to separate it into the cuts he wanted.

A half-hour later, out in the swamp, Jud's rifle roared like a clap of thunder. Looking disgusted, Frosty departed to such peace and quiet as he might find under the porch. Andy glanced toward the swamp. Jud had shot. Therefore he had his buck.... In another twenty minutes, he appeared with it.

It was a fair-sized three-year-old. Jud had slit the tendons in the hind legs, thrust the front ones through, fastened them with pegs, and was carrying his buck as Andy would have carried a packsack. But, though the buck probably weighed 140 pounds, Jud was not laboring nor was he the least bit strained. He paused again beside the porch.

"Got one, huh?" Andy greeted him.

"Yep."

"Nice one, too."

"Nice eatin'," Jud grunted. "I take it you know they's owls in the swamp, Andy?"

"Owls?"

"Cat owls," Jud said. "I see six. I'd of shot some but I didn't know as you'd of wanted me to."

"Thanks, Jud."

"Don't mention it," Jud said politely.

He departed with his buck and Andy began to work furiously. "Cat owl" was a local term for great horned owl, and if Jud had seen six during the short time he'd been absent, they had not only invaded the swamp in force but their invasion had occurred since yesterday. Andy nicked his finger, muttered to himself and continued to work feverishly.

One owl in the swamp was a threat. Six could mean only that game had already become scarce in other localities, and the owls were gathering in his swamp to find food. It was true that, in winter, much small game did seek a refuge in the swamp and, for that very reason, it had more than its winter-time quota of great horned owls and other predators. This early in the season, Andy's muskrats must be the very lure that was attracting them. He had feared just such an invasion, and now he must fight it.

He wrapped the venison in flour sacking, hung the portions in his shed and closed the door behind him. Finished, he breathed a sigh of relief, took his .22 from its rack, filled the magazine, stuck a couple of extra boxes of cartridges in his pocket and started for the swamp.

Frosty, who shuddered at the sight of a shotgun but did not mind the .22, came happily to join him. Andy was rational again. They could take up their partnership where it had been broken off. Tail erect and even whiskers seeming to quiver with joy, Frosty trotted by Andy's side.

Andy set a direct course for the nearest trees. He searched eagerly, hoping he would not find what he feared he would, and optimism leaped in his breast when he saw nothing.

Then an owl, a huge bird with a mighty spread of wings, labored up from a slough with a muskrat in its talons. Andy leveled his rifle, holding it steady, even while he tried to conquer the sick feeling in the pit of his stomach. Compared to some other birds, the owls are not swift fliers and this one was furthered slowed by the burden it carried. It was possible to pick it out of the air with a rifle, but Andy held his fire because, obviously, the owl intended to light in one of the trees. A sitting shot was not sporting, but there was no question of sport connected with this and a sitting shot was far more certain.

The owl dipped gracefully toward a tree and Andy followed with the rifle sights. At exactly the right moment, he squeezed the trigger. The vicious little rifle spat its leaden death and the owl dropped limply. He lay tumbled on the ground, talons still imbedded in the muskrat, when Andy reached him. It was a grip of steel, so powerful that the boy had to use the point of his knife to disengage each talon separately.

Andy skinned the still-warm muskrat, knowing as he did so that the pelt would bring less than a good price because the owl's talons had pierced it. But it was something salvaged.

The next owl was a dodging gray shape that winged erratically over the swamp grass, more than six hundred feet away. Andy leveled his rifle, sighted and shot. He shot a second time . . . and a third. On the third shot, a gray feather detached itself from the bird and floated gracefully downwards. But the shot also warned the owl. He dipped out of sight.

Hearing something in the grass that interested him, Frosty went to investigate. Andy strode grimly toward the next grove of trees. He scored a clean miss on an owl perched in a tree, then brought down one in flight. Quickly, he reloaded his little rifle. It was better than the shotgun for such hunting, partly because shotgun shells were so much more expensive and partly because the shotgun was limited in range. He would certainly have killed the owl in the tree had he had the shotgun, but probably he would have merely wounded the pair he had brought down and even owls deserved better than that.

Far off, hopelessly out of range, Andy saw two owls in the hollow sycamore that overlooked the slough where the five muskrats lived. He stooped to crawl. When he was within rifle shot, he raised cautiously above the swamp grass—to see the sycamore empty. He muttered to himself. He did not think that he had frightened the owls, for they were incredibly bold. Doubtless they'd gone off to hunt, and almost surely they were hunting muskrats.

Rising, Andy walked to the hollow sycamore and cradled the rifle in the crook of his arm while he leaned against it. Five minutes later, a muskrat emerged from an underwater burrow, surfaced and swam in little circles. Only his head and back broke water. He regarded Andy with beady little eyes. Although less than ten feet away, the muskrat considered himself safe because he was in the water.

The owl came so silently and so eerily that, somehow, it seemed to have materialized out of thin air. Gliding over the slough, it took the swimming muskrat in both claws and never missed a wing beat as it flew on. Andy gasped. He leveled the rifle and shot five times, but the gathering dusk made his aim uncertain and again he missed. Andy's brain reeled.

Naturally ferocious, the raiding owls were ten times as fierce and ten times as dangerous as they ever were otherwise because they were also desperately hungry. This one must have seen Andy, but the presence of an armed man had not prevented it from taking a muskrat that was not even a pebble's toss away.

Andy glared at the darkening sky, as though his fierce will to hold back the night and let him continue hunting owls would somehow grant time for so long. But approaching night would not be stopped, and he could do nothing before another morning. However, the owls could and would hunt. All night long the muskrats in the swamp would be at their mercy—and they had no mercy!

Andy trailed tiredly back to his house. He found Frosty on the porch, let him in and nibbled at a supper for which he had neither taste nor desire. Unless something came to his aid, he was ruined and he knew it. One man alone could not turn back the tide of owls. Given one more week, they would take every muskrat from every slough.

Back in the swamp with daylight the next morning, Andy shot two owls almost before night's curtain lifted. Hunting, he got three more and missed four. Then, shortly before noon, the wind began to scream. Just before dusk, it lulled, and that night Andy looked happily at his frosted windows. He had to go outside to read the thermometer, but he'd have walked five miles to discover that it was twelve degrees below zero.

The following morning, every pond and every slough wore a safe armor of ice.

It was an extraordinary winter. Neither mild nor severe, it skipped the usual January thaw completely and lingered on almost as it had started. Except for the one severe cold snap that froze the swamp, the temperature dropped to zero or below only on a few scattered days. However, on two days alone did it climb into the fifties. Most of the time it lingered at a few degrees below or a few above the freezing point.

The customary snows did not fall. The deepest, only about three inches, came shortly before the temperature reached the fifties and much of it melted then. Otherwise, there were only dustings of snow. Thus, though there was tracking most of the time, snowshoes were never needed.

For Andy it was a wonderful, peaceful time, which was further distinguished by being The Winter of the Big Bonanza.

Few of the town dwellers were so old-fashioned as to have coal furnaces. Strictly in tune with modern trends, they used oil or gas. But the ways of the forefathers are not that easily forsaken, and, though the town dwellers also considered this strictly in keeping with progress, a great many of them wanted fireplaces. They served no practical purpose because their houses were always warm enough anyhow. But the fireplaces did fill a spiritual need, and having them, the townsmen wanted fuel to burn in them. Naturally, nobody with a fireplace would consider burning anything except wood.

A fuel-dealer in town had given the Casman brothers an order for 300 cords of fireplace wood, to be picked up at the Casman farm and paid for at six dollars a cord. Even though the same dealer was selling it in town for twelve dollars a cord, it was still a good deal. Jud and Ira, remembering that Andy had invited them to participate in his muskrat ranch on a share basis, invited him to do the same with their wood. Three men were needed for supplying the wood. The Casmans had several acres of yellow birch which they wanted to clear for additional pasture anyhow, also the horses to haul the poles and the machinery for sawing them. The Casmans were to keep one third of the payment. They would split the remaining two thirds three ways with Andy.

Andy accepted happily, for he had already taken as many mink and fox pelts as he could safely take and leave enough for re-stocking. His trappings throughout the rest of the winter would have been confined to taking bobcats and weasels, upon both of which there was a bounty, and he'd have been lucky to earn one hundred dollars. Since his muskrats were safe beneath the ice, a routine patrol sufficed for the swamp. He could do that on Sunday. Anyway, he liked to cut wood.

For the first week, armed with razor-sharp axes that were kept that way by frequent honing, the three of them attacked the grove of yellow birch. Then, while Ira and Andy set up the gasoline-powered buzz saw, Ira used his own horses to drag the wood in to them. When they had enough to keep them busy for a while, he felled and trimmed more trees alone. Except for Sundays, which the Casmans always observed, even though they did not do it in church, the trio worked hard every day from dawn to dusk. As a result, wood piled up fast.

One afternoon, Andy glanced at the sun, calculated that they could work at least one more hour and picked up one end of a birch pole, while Ira took the other. Co-ordinating their actions perfectly, for they had been working together a long while, they swung it into the cradle. Ira had taken the saw end, and Andy was just as happy. The whirling saw, kept as sharp as the axes, could scream its way through a twelve-inch tree in a couple of clock ticks—and through a man's hand in considerably less time! But Ira, who had been handling the business end of a buzz saw ever since he'd been old enough to work, had yet to receive his first nick.

The pair finished the log, took another, and at exactly the right time Jud came in from the wood lot. The three of them worked to arrange the tumbled pile of wood in neat cords, eight feet long by four feet high, and so well did they know what they were doing that, by the time they were finished, it lacked only a few minutes of being too dark to work any more.

Ira solemnly regarded the results of their day's labor. "Twenty mo' cords to go," he announced. "We finish early nex' week."

"Jest in time," Jud said. "Breakup's comin', an' them town folk won't want wood then."

"How do you know the breakup's coming?" Andy challenged him.

"My rheumatiz changed."

"Twon't be much of a breakup," Ira murmured. "Ain't enough snow fo' that. I mistrust 'twill be a puny season' fo' crops, less'n we get a heap o' spring rains."

"There'll be water in the swamp," Andy said.

"Allus some theah," Ira conceded. "How's yo' mushrats doin', Andy?"

Andy hid his instinctive smile. He'd been working with the Casmans all winter, and this was the first time either had asked about his muskrats. In the hills, a man's business was strictly his own.

"I figure the owls cleaned out five colonies," Andy said, "and probably got an animal or two from others. But since I've been able to walk on the ice, I've found seven colonies that I hadn't even known about. They're on little bits of slough arms that I couldn't even reach before."

"Any owls theah now?"

"About the usual winter's supply. I haven't been shooting any since the freeze-up because they can't do any great damage. No sense in shooting anything at all for the sake of killing."

"Tha's right," Jud agreed. "But won't they raise the dickens when the breakup comes?"

"Not too much," Andy said. "Birds will be coming back and everything else will move more. The owls will scatter. Well, see you Monday."

"Shuah thing," Jud said gravely.

"Shuah thing," Ira echoed.

Andy walked homeward and Frosty met him. For the first week, the big cat had accompanied his partner to the wood

lot and happily explored new country while trees were felled.
But, though Frosty did not mind the thudding of axes, he
disliked the screeching buzz saw even more cordially than
blasting rifles and shotguns. He was happy to stay near Andy
nights and to accompany him on Sunday patrols into the
swamp.

They went together the next day, walking safely on ice
and frozen earth. The five colonies that had been ravished—
and Andy was sure that owls had raided them—were easy to
locate. The tops of all muskrat houses protruded above the
ice that locked them in, but these five had fallen into disrepair and the winds were scattering them. All the rest of the
houses were firm and sound.

The next week, Andy finished his job with the Casmans
and, just as Jud had predicted, the breakup followed. It was
no violent change but a soft and gentle thing. One day the
temperature climbed to near-summer heights and remained
there for three days. It wiped out the snow and presently
it took the ice, too. Because there had been little snow and
not much spring run-off, except for the thaw, there was
almost no change in the swamp.

Andy resumed his daily patrols. The owls were still
present and, as Andy discovered when one plucked a rabbit
from under his very nose, still ravenous. But muskrats that
had been ice-bound for weeks were frantic for a taste of
fresh food. They swarmed out of dens and houses to dig in
the mud for anything succulent. Their very eagerness made
them careless. Andy shot a bobcat with a muskrat in its
mouth, found where a great horned owl had taken one, and
a fox another. But there was no great wave of predators
immediately.

Another week elapsed before he knew definitely that

something was seriously wrong. The sign left by digging muskrats was easy to see, and after a week, in eight separate colonies, there was not only no fresh sign but the houses were falling into disrepair. Andy redoubled his efforts, going into the swamp with daylight and staying until dark. This predator was a complete mystery. It left neither tracks nor sign, and the only evidence that it had struck at all was another colony that no longer contained muskrats. Andy, who had thought he knew everything there was to know about the swamp, gave up.

He did not understand this, but Joe Wilson might be able to give him some good advice, for Joe was very wise. An hour before dark, Andy climbed the path leading to the road and struck out toward town. He had walked no more than half a mile when he saw a horseman coming toward him.

It was Luke Trull, whose eyes were cold and whose smile was colder. He passed without speaking, but for a full two minutes Andy stood rooted. Then he turned slowly back toward his house. The Trull-Gates feud, with Luke and himself as sole participants, was about to be renewed, for, in addition to his usual disreputable clothing, Luke wore a muskrat-skin hat!

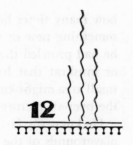

12

DEEP SAND

        Ten minutes after Andy left, Frosty went into the swamp. He had his full growth now, and his twelve pounds were distributed perfectly over a near-perfect frame. Lithe muscles were under exact control of a brain that, naturally fast, had been further sharpened by the dangers to which he had been exposed. Because he was very sure of himself and what he could do, Frosty disdained to hide from even the great horned owls, unless he felt like it. He would fight anything anywhere, if fighting seemed the wisest course. But he would hide, if hiding best served the ends he wanted to achieve. He was never guided by anything save his own intelligence, and he met each situation according to circumstances.

        Not especially hungry, tonight he was in the mood to accept a tempting tidbit should one come his way. Most of all, he wanted to wander and explore, for his feline curiosity never had been and never would be satisfied. No matter

how many times he went into the swamp, he always found
something new or some new aspect to something old. And
he had prowled the swamp so much that, though the rabbit
or muskrat that lived its whole life in one comparatively
small area might know that are better than he, Frosty grasped
the over-all picture more completely than anything else.

He knew the favorite grazing grounds, sleeping places and
playgrounds of the deer. Every muskrat colony—and Frosty
knew of two which even Andy had not yet found—he had
visited time after time and he was aware of the exact number
of muskrats in each. He was acquainted with every mink,
fox, bobcat, raccoon and coyote in the swamp, and he could
go directly to their home dens or the place where each indi-
vidual preferred to hunt. He knew the trees or copses of
trees which the great horned owls preferred, and where the
grouse were inclined to roost. Frosty was familiar with those
places where rabbits and mice were most abundant. He had
trod every safe trail and visited most of the hiding places.

Knowing all this, the swamp still fascinated him because
it was never static. There was always change, and, next to
his partnership with Andy, keeping aware and abreast of
those changes was the most important business in Frosty's
life.

The first night Luke Trull entered the swamp, Frosty had
known of his presence a half-hour later. Luke's trespassing
angered him greatly, and he still would harm the man if
he could find a way to do so. He had not discovered the way,
and it was far from prudent to attack even a hated man
unless there was every chance of winning the fight. Because
he did want to discover what Luke was about, Frosty followed him until he knew his exact schedule.

He habitually came just a few minutes after gray twilight

shaded into deep night. Invariably he entered the swamp by wading a shallow, hard-bottomed slough four hundred yards from Andy's house. His equipment was always the same, five number one traps that he carried in his left hand and a club clutched in his right. An empty packsack hung loosely over his shoulders and there was a knife at his belt.

He knew the safe trails so well that he needed no light to guide himself, but he carried a small flashlight to carry on his affairs, once he was within the swamp—and his affairs concerned the muskrat colonies. Though he did not understand it, Frosty had watched what he did there.

When Luke approached a colony, the muskrats were sure to be digging for bulbs in the bank. They always fled when he came, but they seldom went farther than the center of the pond or slough in which they lived. Luke used his flashlight to see where they had been digging. Then, depending on what he saw, he set one or more traps. The traps were strung on flexible wires, slipped through the ring in the chain. Wooden pegs prevented their sliding off. Luke cast one end of his wire into the slough or pond, tied the other to any convenient root, tree or shrub, set his traps and went to another colony.

Sometimes the muskrats came back as soon as Luke left. Sometimes they were cautious for an hour or more. But they always came and they were always trapped. When they were, they dived frantically into the water which, hitherto, had provided a safe refuge. The trap chain, sliding along the wire, was invariably stopped by the wooden peg. Since no muskrat in trouble would ever think of turning toward land, they continued their efforts to get into the water until they drowned.

Coming back, Luke picked up the drowned muskrats,

placed them in the packsack, took his traps and was out of the swamp well before daylight. He had never taken more than five muskrats on any one night. But neither had he taken any less, and he had visited the swamp for seven consecutive nights.

Frosty expected him again tonight, but he was not particulary worried about the man's possible appearance because he could take care of himself. In the dark, he could always get out of any human's way. They never even seemed to know that he was around.

The big cat faced into the brisk north wind. Spring, showing her face briefly, had only wanted to tantalize the winter-weary. The wind was as cold as it had been most winter nights and there were a few snowflakes, but not enough to whiten the ground and retain tracks. Undaunted by the cold wind, that could ruffle but not penetrate his thick fur, Frosty gave his attention to a sound that was borne to his ears.

The noise was made by a roosting bird that fluttered its wings as it changed position. It was not a bird that had been in the swamp last night. A venturesome robin, impatient to be away from the south and back at the all-important business of building a nest and rearing a family, had taken a chance on the weather. Now, huddling miserably on a naked aspen, it was probably wishing it hadn't. Searching in vain for warmth, the robin shifted again.

Grown a bit hungry, Frosty stalked the tree. He advanced so artfully that few things would have taken fright, so it was not Frosty's presence that launched the robin from its perch. It was the cold wind. The robin fluttered off into the darkness, to see if there might not be a warmer roost.

Always angry when a victim eluded him, Frosty stood

with one forepaw uplifted and lashed his tail. Even though experience had taught him that there would be nights when all luck leaned on the side of whatever he hunted, stalking and missing always stung. He hunted to kill, he was satisfied with nothing else, and missing the robin seemed to intensify his hunger.

Frosty abandoned exploring in favor of determined hunting. He headed for a thicket in which several rabbits had wintered and crouched quietly beside a runway. He was hungry and growing hungrier, but he was also patient. He'd stay here for hours, if necessary, and sooner or later a rabbit would come along the runway. But he'd waited only minutes when one hopped toward him. Tense and ready to spring, the black cat did not move.

The rabbit was almost within springing distance when a great horned owl swooped to catch it. Frosty spat his anger and leaped to attack, but the owl was airborne and he fell short by inches. There came the sounds of thumping feet as the other rabbits, finally aware of an enemy in their midst, told each other about it and sought the safety of burrows.

Frosty lashed his tail and glared. Sooner or later, the rabbits would come out again. He would get one if he waited, but he was too hungry to wait. He set his course toward the high knob upon which the hollow sycamore grew. There were a few rabbits in the scrub there. Frosty laid his ambush, waited, made a kill and started to eat.

Almost as soon as he began his meal, he stopped eating. His ears informed him that Luke Trull was coming. Unwilling to abandon his hard-won dinner, Frosty held perfectly still. Luke set his traps, went on, and Frosty finished eating. He washed himself thoroughly and felt a little sleepy.

He'd have a nap before prowling any more, and since he

was going to rest, he might as well do it out of the wind. The hollow sycamore, in which he'd slept several times, offered shelter. Frosty padded to the hollow and entered.

He halted abruptly when one of Luke's muskrat traps snapped on his paw, but he did not panic. Frosty touched the trap with his nose and he tried to take a bite from it. The steel was hard and unyielding; if he continued to bite it, he'd do nothing except shatter his jaws. Therefore he would not bite. This was a time for planning.

The plan, severe enough for anything at all, was ten times as excruciating to a cat's complex nervous system. Frosty still refused to panic. He could not fight this thing, so he must outwit it. He looked at the water and shuddered, then he heard Luke coming back.

Dragging the trap with him, Frosty crawled into the sycamore. He crouched, and mounting fury served to counteract pain. Luke reached the knob. His light flashed once and went out. Frosty stayed quiet, hoping to escape detection by so doing.

But if Luke came near him, he would fight as hard and as viciously as he could.

Andy walked slowly back to his house because there was no need to hurry. Whatever he did from this point on—and he intended to do much—would be carried out in black night, and it still lacked a couple of hours until darkness. As he walked, Andy saw almost everything in a clear light.

He should have known, and he blamed himself for not knowing, that the mysterious predator could be none other than Luke Trull. He had been lulled into a false sense of security by Luke's failure to come raiding all autumn and all winter. But he should also have known that, when he came, Luke would strike at that time when muskrats were most valuable. He was nobody's fool, and naturally he would do his poaching at night.

All this was so unbelievably simple that anyone should have figured it out. Andy had not, but since he finally knew, the problem was far more complex than it appeared on the surface.

He might, he supposed, go to the State Police and say that he had seen Luke Trull wearing a muskrat-skin hat. The police would look at him, and each other, then they would consult their copy of the State Game Laws and point out that muskrat season was open to anyone who had a trapping license and it would be open for two weeks more. No doubt they would remember that he had had previous trouble with Luke, and even on the far-fetched possibility that they took him seriously, no State Trooper would stumble around anyone's swamp at night simply because the swamp's owner had seen someone wearing a muskrat-skin hat.

There was only one way. Turn time backwards for thirty years, and once again a Gates and a Trull would settle their differences in their own way. But Andy knew that he must stop short of killing. Murder, any way one considered it, was murder, and the law had no bearing on the fact that Andy did not want another's blood on his hands. But he looked forward with savage joy to fighting. He would find Luke, beat a confession out of him, and take him to the Police himself. There were a number of reliable witnesses who knew that Andy had bought the muskrats with which the swamp was stocked. If he found Luke poaching, nothing else should be necessary.

At the same time, Andy felt the need for caution.

Luke was a clever person, a cunning schemer who weighed

every action and made it count. Why, when he saw Andy coming, had he not taken off his hat and hidden it? Was it his way of jeering? Letting the hat speak for him, had he announced to Andy that he, Luke Trull, was stealing musk-rats and there was nothing Andy could do about it? Or did he *want* a meeting in the swamp? If so, why? Luke, always willing to do anything at any time as long as it would turn a dollar for himself, seldom got into trouble. He knew the penalty for murder. It was inconceivable that he would come anywhere near risking that penalty. Neither would he fight. But why had he not hidden the hat?

Andy walked on. Luke's reasons for doing or not doing anything no longer made a difference. Andy had to stop him or surrender to him, and he would not surrender. He thought again of his own lack, not exactly of foresight, but failure to act on foresight. Luke had done exactly as Andy had thought he'd do, and explored the swamp thoroughly while Andy languished in jail. Anybody who knew the trails could go into the swamp as easily by night as by day, and the muskrats had never been hurt by any human being. Therefore, they did not fear humans. They'd be easy to trap.

Reaching his house, Andy calmly and methodically un-laced his shoes, took them off, and pulled on rubber boots. He donned a wool jacket, a wool cap that came over his ears, and looked thoughtfully at the gun rack. Andy turned away from it. There must be no killing, and in any fight, passion was apt to overcome good sense. What he had to do, he'd do with his fists.

When darkness was complete, Andy went into the swamp.

His plan was simple. Knowing every colony that still con-tained muskrats, he would visit each. If Luke were in the swamp tonight, they'd meet. With only a brief glance at Four-Leaf and Clover, since they were so near the house Luke would know better than to bother them, Andy went on to Dead Man's Slough. He swerved to investigate some colonies in another part of the swamp and swung back. Three hours later, a half-hour before midnight, he thought he saw a light.

Andy stopped in his tracks and fixed intent eyes on the place at which he thought the light had originated. For a second he turned his eyes away, then glanced back. There was no light now and perhaps there never had been any. His imagination could be playing tricks, but Andy turned away from the course he'd set himself and went directly towards the high knob upon which the hollow sycamore grew. He thought he'd seen the light there, and there were still muskrats in that slough.

Nearing the high knob, he stopped to look and listen. But the north wind, still carrying a few snowflakes on its screaming wings, drowned all other noises and there was little light. Very cautiously, Andy continued to advance. He climbed the knob and leaned against a small aspen.

There was a sudden, jarring pain in his head and a galaxy of bright lights danced before his eyes. He staggered, tried to hold himself up by gripping the aspen, and for a second he succeeded. Presently he was aware of pain.

Andy opened bewildered eyes. The last he remembered, he had been holding onto an aspen and looking about. Now he lay prone, hands and feet bound with wire, and a flashlight was shining in his face. Somebody said something he could not hear and he closed his eyes. Then he heard,

"I thought ye'd come, Gates."

Andy reopened his eyes to see Luke Trull, still wearing

his disreputable clothing and the muskrat-skin hat, looking down at him. Andy shivered. There was about Luke the same lethal coldness that there is about a rattlesnake just before it strikes. Luke spoke again,

"Ye hit me, Gates."

"Let me loose, you fool!"

Luke grinned mirthlessly, and in the faint light his eyes seemed to glow. He said,

"I wanted ye to know what was goin' to happen. Tha's why I din' do it afore."

"Didn't do what?"

"Put ye in the slough."

"They'll get you for it, Luke."

Luke's grin widened. "Ye know better'n that. Ye know well's I do that more'n one man lies in these deep sand sloughs, my own pappy 'mongst 'em, an' a Gates put him thar. Ye allus mess 'round this swamp, an' what'll folks think when ye jest don't come out?"

"You're putting your head in a noose!"

"No I hain't, Gates. No I hain't. An' ye did hit me. Nobody hits Luke Trull an'," he chuckled, "I thought ye'd be in the swamp after ye saw my hat. How do you like it, Gates? Made it myself with two pelts f'om your swamp."

"You're talking like an idiot!"

"Idiot? I got thirty fi' o' your mushrats so far an' fo' here," he indicated the packsack. "Now I see that I got me 'nother in the hollow tree. I'll let ye see me pull it out an' kill it, Gates, afore I roll ye in the slough an' let ye sink in the deep sand."

He walked toward and bent near the hollow sycamore while Andy made a mighty effort to loose his bonds. He strained, felt the flexible wire give, and knew that he could free himself. If he could only do it in time . . .

He saw Luke pull at the taut wire and heard a spitting snarl. Fury incarnate, Frosty came out of the hollow and sprang straight to Luke's head. He clawed and scratched while he continued to spit.

Luke stood up, waved his hands like windmill blades, lost his footing, and tumbled backwards into the slough. Andy gasped, continuing to strain at the wire that bound him, even while he remained unable to take his eyes from the drama being enacted before his eyes. The slough was quicksand, and as far as Andy knew, it was bottomless. But a good swimmer, even a fully clothed one, who knew what he was doing could cross it safely. Andy sighed in relief.

Luke was a good swimmer, and obviously he both realized his danger and knew what he was doing. Only the muskrat-skin hat, leaving a trailing V-curl behind it, broke water as he dog-paddled very slowly and very cautiously. He would make it all right.

The thing that came did so with uncanny silence. A great horned owl that had not been there a second before was there now, hovering over what could be nothing except a swimming muskrat. It struck, and rose with Luke's hat in its talons. Then it was gone.

Andy struggled frantically to free himself, but each second was an hour long and each minute a day. Finally working bleeding hands from the wire, he loosed his legs and rose. The slough was empty, with not even a ripple to show that anything had ever been on it. After two minutes, Andy turned toward Frosty, who growled warningly but let his partner depress the trap spring and free his paw.

Frosty fell to cleaning himself. With a prayer in his heart,

again Andy searched the slough. But all he saw was a pair
of swimming muskrats. At least two had survived, just as
two must have survived in other sloughs. The muskrats
paid no attention to death, for their function was life. They
would build houses, dig dens, and eventually they would
overspread the swamp.

The muskrats dived and only bubbles rose.

JIM KJELGAARD

was born in New York City. Happily enough, he was still in the pre-school age when his father decided to move the family to the Pennsylvania mountains. There young Jim grew up among some of the best hunting and fishing in the United States. He says: "If I had pursued my scholastic duties as diligently as I did deer, trout, grouse, squirrels, etc., I might have had better report cards!"

Jim Kjelgaard has worked at various jobs—trapper, teamster, guide, surveyor, factory worker and laborer. When he was in the late twenties he decided to become a full-time writer. He has succeeded in his wish. He has published several hundred short stories and articles and quite a few books for young people.

His hobbies are hunting, fishing, dogs, and questing for new stories. He tells us: "Story hunts have led me from the Atlantic to the Pacific and from the Arctic Circle to Mexico City. Stories, like gold, are where you find them. You may discover one three thousand miles from home or, as in *The Spell of the White Sturgeon,* right on your own door step." And he adds: "I am married to a very beautiful girl and have a teen-age daughter. Both of them order me around in a shameful fashion, but I can still boss the dog! We live in Phoenix, Arizona."